Leave Our Bones Where They Lay

Aviaq Johnston

Inhabit Media Inc.

For my Anaanatsiak, Lizzie Angusaaruk Kauki

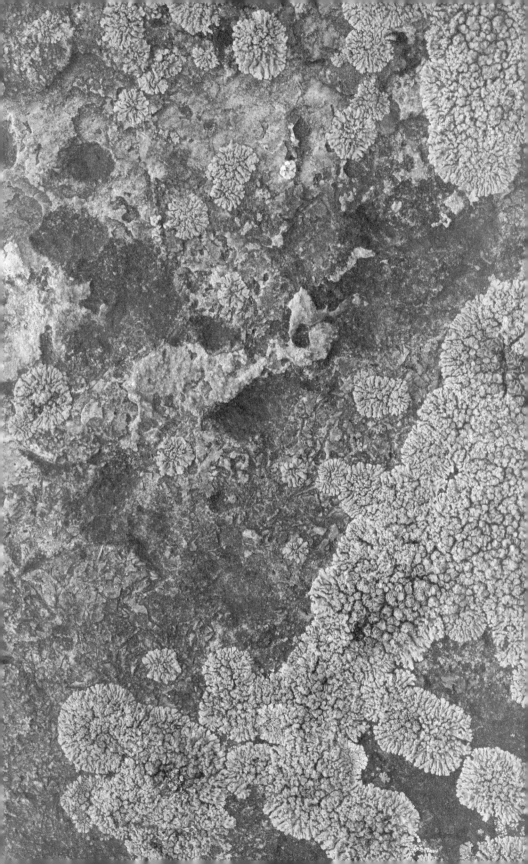

Atii qialirit. Go cry then.
—Ancient Inuit Proverb

Published By Inhabit Media Inc.
www.inhabitmedia.com

Inhabit Media Inc. (Iqaluit) 2434 Paurngaq Cres., Iqaluit, Nunavut, X0A 2H0
(Toronto) 612 Mount Pleasant Rd., Toronto, Ontario, M4S 2M8

Editors: Kelly Ward-Wills and Neil Christopher
Art director: Danny Christopher

We acknowledge the support of the Canada Council for the Arts for
our publishing program.

This project was made possible in part by the Government of Canada.

ISBN: 978-1-77227-589-6

Printed in Canada

Canada

Canada Council   Conseil des Arts
for the Arts   du Canada

Library and Archives Canada Cataloguing in Publication

Title: Leave our bones where they lay / Aviaq Johnston.
Names: Johnston, Aviaq, author
Identifiers: Canadiana 20250258064 | ISBN 9781772275896 (softcover)
Subjects: LCGFT: Short stories.
Classification: LCC PS8619.O4848 L43 2025 | DDC C813/.6—dc23

Content Warning:

This book mentions death, suicide, violence, alcohol and substance abuse, and other colonial trauma. Please take care of yourself while reading. *Aiin.*

The Five Inuit Seasons

Ukiuq – Winter

Upirngassaaq – Early Spring

Upirngaaq – Spring

Aujaq – Summer

Ukiaq – Fall

Table of Contents

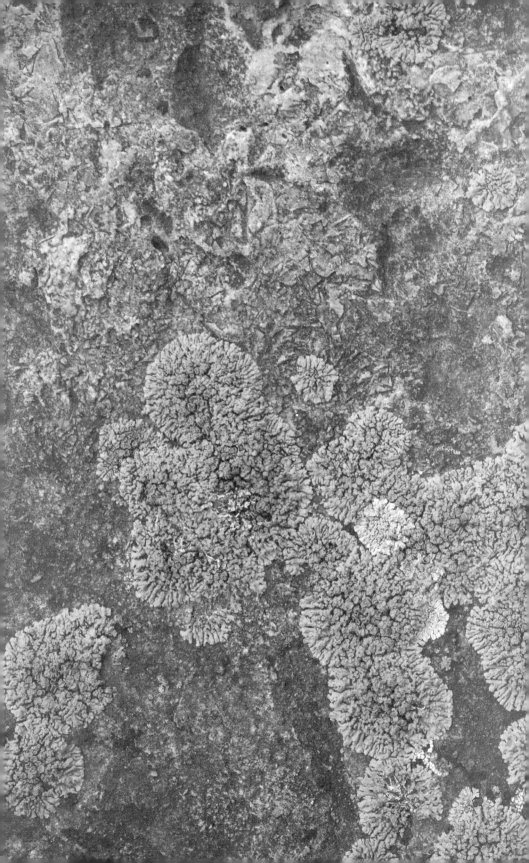

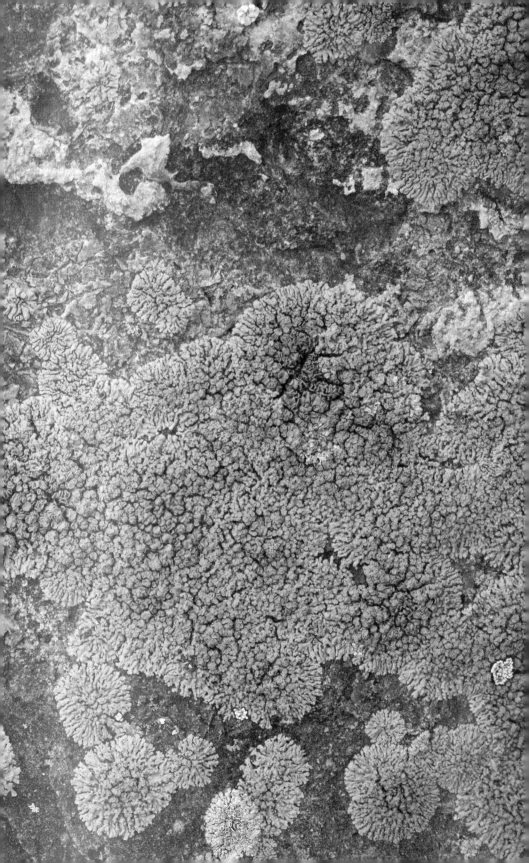

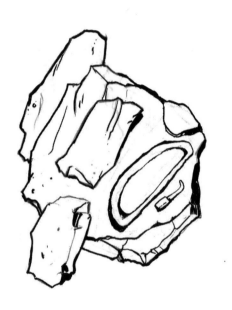

Ukiuq | Winter

I.

It was not a common area to run into another person. The trail was too treacherous for a Ski-Doo to get through in the winter, and the inlet too shallow and full of boulders for boats in the summer. The tides were extreme, making it so that the ice formed into an unnavigable terrain of jagged edges, dangerous cracks, and inexplicable crevasses. Crumbling cliffs surrounded the inlet, except for a narrow path that could only be found by those who knew of it. Even then, the snow gathered deeply and uncharacteristically soft, making the hike from inland equally difficult. Rocks often fell unpredictably from the cliff face. A relentless wind tore throughout the area, swiping away any trails and tracks that may be left behind by someone who'd been brave enough to venture forward.

Everything about the place warned a person to proceed no further, to turn back home and wipe what was seen from memory.

Yet, during the mid-point of each of the five Inuit seasons, there was always a hearth with an old, stone *qulliq* the size of a large roast pan lit in the centre of the gravel beach. Skeletons of small animals littered the shale rock shoreline, left by roosting hawks and falcons. The lamp was lit by an old hunter who'd been coming here for decades, since his own father had shown him the location in his youth.

The old hunter was short and skinny, with a greying, thick moustache upon his upper lip. It'd taken decades to grow it that thick and he had no intention of shaving it. He also wore tinted glasses, the same pair he'd worn for thirty years, not quite as effective as they used to be, his vision having worsened over time. He was in his sixties now, but he didn't look it. He was the type of timeless man who hadn't changed at all in four decades, his age only betrayed by the outdated look of the things he wore. He was spry, able to traverse the various protections the shoreline had put up in defence, a rifle slung across his back.

He waited, as he always did, for his companion to emerge from a trick of the light in the rugged crevices of the cliffside.

His companion came to the fire unpredictably, sometimes only once a year, or once a decade. Sometimes one season after another. The consequences of the old hunter skipping the ceremony and the companion appearing to an unlit fire far outweighed the difficulty of the journey to light it.

When the moon reached the highest it could at each time of year, whether in the light of day or in the middle of the night, the figure appeared from the shadows and cracks. The spirit materialized into an approximation of a person, but their eyes and mouth were configured vertically. A being of nightmares, but the old hunter was no longer afraid of the spirit's presence. When they'd first met, the old hunter—back then only a child—had hardly slept because of the terror he'd felt. Now, they greeted each other as friends.

"Jupi," said the figure.

"Kipik," said the old hunter.

A moment of silence as Kipik settled into the space, slowly forming their outline into a more static shape.

Kipik's voice was wheezy, the lungs of a creature hundreds of years old, deprived of breath. Hearing the spirit's voice always prompted Jupi to clear his own throat.

Kipik began, "It is always a pleasure to see you again—"

"Likewise," Jupi replied.

"—Yet, I notice you still haven't brought a successor." A smile formed on Kipik's lips. Though vertical, Jupi could see that it was wry—disappointed even. "You know, you are aging, old friend."

Jupi raised his eyebrows. "*Iilaak.* I know."

"So, why haven't you brought one of your sons to see me again?" Kipik asked. "I've known you since you were ten. Your sons must be grown and have children of their own by now."

Jupi, again, agreed by raising his brows. He cleared his throat again, trying to figure out what to say next. "My, uh," he faltered, shook his head and coughed. "My sons are just not interested in coming out here."

Kipik's eyes narrowed, "You do know what will happen if you pass on without securing another to take your place, yes?"

"Yes," Jupi agreed, though he was unsure of the consequences if he thought about it. Maybe once, when he was much, much younger, he did know. The memory was long faded by now.

Kipik was ancient and unhurried. They waited for Jupi to elaborate.

"I will bring one of them next time," Jupi conceded.

For now, that was enough to sate the old spirit. An expression not too far off from a smile formed over their face. It was almost friendly, but with a tinge of sinister reverence.

"*Ii*, okay." The smile widened. "*Atii*. Tell me a story."

Sanna

This is a story of a woman we do not speak the name of. She was once a beautiful young woman, so beautiful that men from near and far would make the journey to meet with her father and make marriage proposals. See, she was not only beautiful, but she was supposedly exquisitely skilled, her waterproof stitches were none to compete with, the lilt of her singing coaxing all to serenity, her duty to look after a camp never questioned. She lived alone with her father and her dog, and she was content to stay there, refusing all the proposals.

"Taima. *Stop.*" *Kipik interrupted*, "*You have told me this one before.*"

"Aakkai," *Jupi denied*, "*I told you a different story, about Nuliajuk, but this one is about Sanna. It's similar, but they are not the same story.*"

"*It does not make it a different story if it is about the same Being.*"

Jupi considered. "But it is different. In this one, she is impregnated by a dog, and her father becomes angry and drowns her, but she becomes a powerful spirit and gives birth to her half-dog, half-fish, half-human children. And she becomes a giant woman at the bottom of the ocean, and if she so much as moves one of her knuckles, it creates a tidal wave on the ocean's surface."

"You have told me her story before. Even if it became different over time and place. The bones are the same. Tell me something else."

"Okay," Jupi said, deflated. He scoured his mind for another . . .

Kaugjagjuk

In the winter, people often stumbled upon a young boy sleeping in their *iglu* porch with their sled dogs. It was the warmest spot for an orphaned boy with no family. He was known to be a wretch, unskilled and unable to provide for anyone, let alone himself. People fed him scraps, and sometimes he'd have to viciously wrestle with the dogs for his share of food. His name was Kaugjagjuk.

"Ack! Taannattauq," Kipik interrupted again. "You have told me this one also!"

"No, I never'd!" Jupi argued.

"You've forgotten?" Kipik asked. "My memory is better than yours. It was the very first story you told me, when you were twelve years old."

"No, it was my father who told the story," Jupi retorted, "I'm sure of it."

"It was not your father. He told me the story of Kaugjagjuk when he was a young man, too. You mix yourself up. You and he were closely intwined, sometimes telling the stories together, since you came here together for decades until he died."

"I suppose this is why a successor would be helpful," Jupi said.

"Among other things."

"Okay," Jupi said, deep in thought once more. "I have a story."

Maniittuq

The ride to the cabin was long, but leisurely. It was mostly smooth, with only one patch of rough packed tidal ice, which was reasonably maneuverable with the snowmobile. Once through the treacherous trail, there was a long climb up a steep hill, then a long winding trail down. After that, it flattened and straightened out for forty kilometres or so, through the valleys of rolling, rocky hills.

There was only one area where Saa hesitated, and parked the snowmobile for a moment to gather her bearings. It was a channel in which the current was strong and the ice rarely formed thick enough in various areas, sometimes making it difficult to spot. Just on the other side of the channel was Maniittuq, a gorgeous bay interspersed with small islands and an abundant river flowing with Arctic char. Saa and her father had gone through this area many times together, it was unavoidable—the last stretch before finally reaching the cabin—but it was her first time going alone.

She could see her father's trail from the day before, slightly windswept but easy enough to follow. They had discussed this part of the journey quite extensively, going over it in meticulous detail to ensure Saa would feel confident in her passage; what she should do when she reached the channel, what signs to keep an eye out for, to be vigilant, and to take deep breaths before proceeding.

Saa looked around, spotting animal tracks close by. She walked over to them to try to recognize what animal had created them. As easy as second nature, she knew that they were polar bear tracks. The area was teeming with the animals. She squinted her eyes—there was something odd about them.

With closer inspection, she could make out the tracks of another animal inset with the bear's tracks. These she was more unfamiliar with, and she racked her brain for what they could be. Not big enough to be a wolf, but larger than a fox, something in between.

It took a moment for her to pinpoint it. *Qavvik!* A wolverine.

A chill ran over her spine. She'd been told stories about this area since her father had decided to build his cabin here, many of which involved a wolverine roaming the area, and a woman screaming or crying from over the hillsides or roving the shoreline and preying on those who crossed her path. Many of the stories led to the belief that the wolverine and the woman were synonymous with one another.

On top of that, the polar bear tracks were deeply concerning. They were fresh. The cabin had been standing for five years now, and it was notoriously known for being broken into by polar bears at least two or three times a year. Sometimes more. Despite the door and windows getting boarded up with plywood every time they left, and all traces of food and trash being brought home at the end of every visit. They'd often return to find the sheets of wood flung off or askew, the door opened wide, and the cabin slowly filling with snow.

Worry spread into Saa's belly, and she got back on her snowmobile to finish the journey. She realized that she hadn't contacted her father on the VHF radio before heading out. The last she'd heard from him was the night before, when he let the family know that he'd made it safely to the cabin.

Her father had left after work yesterday, taking an extra day off for the spring long weekend. Saa, on the other hand, felt like she couldn't take the time off, after missing several days due to hangovers and other sicknesses that were more likely due to the lethargy of depression than anything else.

Now, she just wished she'd gone ahead with him. Would she have gotten fired? Probably not. Just another fact-finding meeting with HR, a slap on the wrist, disappointment from her coworkers and supervisors, but nothing drastic.

Her worry propelled her forward. She sped through the channel at full speed, noticing the slushy patches of ice at the last minute and swerving around them. She made it to the end of the channel fine, if a little panicked, her heart racing.

The journey ended with a last bend around a small peninsula, and in the little bay, the cabin rested on a plateau on the hill. Maniittuq was named for the rough terrain across the range of hills throughout the area. There was very little tide here, so the pack ice was easy to traverse and drive through. She could see her father's snowmobile parked next to the cabin, but no smoke wafting from the chimney. The plywood had been taken off the windows and safely leaned against the cabin, not torn off by bears.

But as she closed the distance, her angle on the cabin changed and she could see the cabin door opened wide.

"Dad!" She yelled. "Dad?"

No answer. *Maybe he's gone on a walk over the hill? Maybe he just didn't close the door properly? Maybe it was too hot inside and he needed to cool down?*

But as she shut her machine off, there was a deafening silence.

"Dad?"

There was no reply.

Saa swung her rifle off her shoulder and loaded it, switching off the safety, and rushed into the cabin. It was freezing inside, the diesel heater gone cold. Snow had been trailed in by an obviously gigantic creature. Supplies were strewn about, her father's grub box and cooler torn apart, bits of the foam mattress littered, the Colman stove bent out of shape and leaking naphtha. An old can of Pepsi left on the floor with holes as big as thumbs bitten into it by fangs that could rip a human body apart.

No blood. So maybe her father was out hunting by foot. His rifle was gone, too. She lowered her own rifle.

She spotted the VHF and grabbed hold of the mic. "Elena, *tusaaviit*? Elena, are you listening?" But there was only static on the line. She spoke into the mic again, "*Tusaqsauvungaa?* Can you hear me?"

There was only static. Saa didn't understand the contraption well enough to know whether the signal was not working or if it was just that nobody was listening. Perhaps the wind or bear had jostled the antenna or wires outside? She didn't even know if that was something the VHF needed, her father had always been there to fix it if something was wrong. The skills to figure out what was wrong were not in her wheelhouse.

She marched back outside, screamed, "DAD!" only to hear her voice echoed back.

Saa slung her rifle back over her shoulders, unstrapped her pack from the back of her snowmobile, and brought it inside. She started the diesel heater to start warming up the cabin, took off her parka, and went through the bag, taking out a granola bar and scarfing it down. Underneath her parka, she was wearing a light down-filled coat, and her bib-style overall snow pants were tucked into warm boots. She grabbed extra bullets, stashing them in one of her many pockets.

She left the cabin to keep warming up, checked the ground for tracks, and found her father's footprints, as well as the meandering tracks of the polar bear following. She marched off in pursuit.

The tracks of both her father and the bear led uphill to high ground. This made sense to Saa—if she hadn't found the footprints, she'd have gone this way anyway. Intermittently, she called out for her father, but never heard a reply. It was eerily quiet, no birds peeping or flying.

At the top of the hill, the wind grew stronger. Saa gazed over the horizon and down the valley, but both her father and the bear were out of sight. Again, she could see the tracks of the two, and she started to follow them.

It was then that she heard the distant sound of a woman crying behind her. Saa stopped, felt the breath catch in her chest. Carefully, she took her rifle from its place slung over her shoulders, and slowly turned around.

Only to see that there was no one there. The sounds of the crying stopped.

For a moment, unbreathing, Saa stood still. Could the sound have been made by a distant bird? But the silence was palpable, as if she had walked into a cloud of nothingness. She opened her jaw, trying to pop her eardrums, to no avail. Holding her breath, she kept making the motions, opening her mouth wide and pushing. The moment of quiet cleared, and she could hear the wind again. She let out a breath and she could hear that, too.

Then another sudden sound. A gunshot, from the direction of her father's tracks.

An alarm set off in Saa's head and she swung herself around, only to see a woman in an old fashioned *amaut* in the middle of the path. With a gasp of terror, Saa shot the rifle at her, but the image of the woman only faded as Saa fell backward into the snow. Her chest heaved, and she looked around frantically in search of the woman.

It was a long time before she calmed herself down, sitting up in the snow. There was still no sign of the woman she'd seen.

Then it all came back to her—the gunshot from the direction her father and the polar bear had travelled. She picked herself up, trying to forget what she had seen, focused only on reaching her father.

She sprinted down the hill, her gun poised in her arms, still loaded with the safety off. Soft patches of snow skewed her balance and she sunk to her knees, her momentum slowed.

The woman's cries were behind her again. Saa did not check, although the crying did not seem as distant as it had earlier. Of all the stories she'd heard of this area and the crying woman, none of them had violent or concerning ends, only the lingering feelings of creepiness. No children had been successfully stolen by the crying woman, no one lured to their death. She only ever knew the end of the stories to be of the woman disappearing for long bouts of time and returning occasionally.

"Go away!" Saa yelled, but the crying only grew louder and closer, as if the one making the sound suddenly was behind her. She swore she felt breath on the back of her neck, and Saa swung around, but there was nothing behind her.

When Saa turned back again, the woman was there. She was still filled with terror at the sight, but Saa didn't shoot this time. She stared at the woman's clothing, recognizing now that the amaut she wore was made from wolverine fur. Again, the image of the woman faded.

Saa made her way again, running more carefully, stepping only where the hard snow could bear her weight. Behind her, the woman's cries were no longer the pitiful sobs of a woman's grief. She could make out words now.

"*Taikungaunngilluti!*" and "*Utirululaurit!*" and "*Upanngillugit!*" and "Taima!" "Don't go there!" and "Go back!" and "Don't approach them!" and "Stop!"

Saa tried to continue ignoring the woman's cries, but she hesitated. The stories she'd heard about Maniittuq were often ambiguous, of no real consequence. To her, they had always been anecdotes told by boisterous children for shock value. Once, she was told by a friend that their cousin had seen a blue womanly figure on the shoreline when their family had gone camping here one summer. Another story she'd been told by her high school classmate was that they had seen their brother walking hand in hand with a similar womanly figure, but once they called out to the boy, the woman disappeared and their brother was dazed, without memory.

Saa kept her pace quick-marching down the hill, deep in thought, not acknowledging the cries still lingering behind her. Ghost stories were commonly shared amongst children and teenagers, but "ghost" wasn't the proper term for most of the beings she'd learned about in her culture. Saa turned the words over and over in her head. They were a warning. What beings warned humans back? She could only think of *tarriaksuit* possibly fitting the description, known to her as a peaceful race of beings who lived invisibly.

By the time she reached the valley below, her chest felt hot and painful, her throat dry in a way that no amount of water could quite quench.

She keeled over for a moment, chest heaving. Only a moment to catch her breath before continuing. The woman's cries had faded by now, perhaps sanctioned only on the hillside. She couldn't be sure about the boundaries of spirits, but she often thought that certain spirits stayed confined to one area. In any case, the return of silence was welcome as Saa continued forward.

Why had her father gone so far on foot? Why wouldn't he have used his snowmobile?

She followed the trail onward, a long stint without a sound or sight, just her and the path of her father and the bear before her. Finally, she yelled once again, "Dad!"

But as her echoes faded, she heard again only the whimpering behind her. The sound brought the chill back down her spine, an uncomfortable sigh throughout her body. She continued forward, picking up her pace.

The further she walked, the faster she moved, the crying only became louder and more urgent. Heaving, pathetic sobs, the kind that were inconsolable, ugly sounds. Saa squeezed her eyes shut and tried to cover her ears, but holding the rifle one handed was too heavy and awkward and her head wouldn't stop ringing.

"Stop!" Saa shouted, swinging herself around.

Again, there was no one. The sounds of the cries cut off in the middle of a disgusting, rattling sob.

Hoping the silence would linger once more, Saa turned back to her path, expecting again to see the woman.

But it was not the woman who stood before her this time. It was a snarling wolverine, lunging toward her.

Panicked and off balance, Saa shot her rifle square at the wolverine, and the bullet passed through the animal as it faded into nothingness, just as the crying woman had. The bullet, instead, landed into a man's back.

Saa's ears rang from the shot and she stared at the man as he toppled forward. Stunned, she remained motionless as she kept her eyes on him, willing for his image to disappear as the crying woman's and the wolverine's had, but he stayed there, unmoving.

"Dad?"

Just as before, there was no response.

Her senses returned, a cry bubbled up her throat, "Dad!"

Rushing forward, she found her dad's toppled body, a knife in his hand that he'd been using to butcher the polar bear that had stalked him. She shook his body, but his eyes were open, staring lifelessly at the sky.

II.

After their stories, the companions exchanged brief pleasantries. "Until next time." Kipik bid farewell, faded back into the shadows of the cliff face, once again becoming a being not of earth and bone and skin, but of air and an eternal darkness.

In haste, Jupi left the way he came, wading through the deep and slushy snow, heading inland to where he parked his snowmobile. Once he reached it, he lit a cigarette and took long drags of the smoke. Most of his life, Jupi had met with Kipik, and though he'd grown accustomed to the spirit, he could never overcome the feeling of *after*.

After—after dousing the flames and waiting to make sure Kipik was gone, after trekking through the awful route back, after sitting on his machine to catch his breath—all Jupi ever wanted to do was extinguish anything in his body that kept him alive. He smoked to take the air from his lungs, he went to his cabin and drank a bottle or two of liquor to retreat into a deep oblivion, and he slept until he no longer dreamt of a dark and hopeless future. Sometimes it was only a night to get over it, sometimes it was a week.

It was particularly bad this time. Kipik wanted Jupi's successor.

The subject had come up once or twice before, but never so directly. Jupi had no one who could carry on the tradition, the role that he and his father and his father before him and so on had carried since time immemorial. Jupi had no idea what to do.

A week later, he returned to his small house in town. It was nothing nice, an old rundown structure, allotted to him from the housing corp. It was riddled with haphazard repairs Jupi had done himself, a couple of broken windows boarded up with plywood and garbage bags, roughly plastered holes, flattened cardboard boxes covering up broken tiles in the floor, a stove with only one working burner. He walked in to find his second son watching hockey while seated on the couch that was almost as old as the house itself.

Jupi resisted the urge to sigh. Instead, he removed his glasses as they began to fog up in the warmth of the house.

"Hi, Dad," Mark said. "Montreal versus Boston. Second period."

"Who's winning?" Jupi asked.

"Fuckin' Bruins. Four-O."

There was a flush of the toilet and from the bathroom emerged Jupi's youngest son, Aatami. He produced a tight-lipped smile and in a clipped tone, said, "Hi."

Jupi nodded. He continued to remove his gear, hanging his thick parka, pants, and boots, settling them into the vestibule of the cold porch. The smell of cooking meat wafted from the kitchen. Aatami was making *saattuujaaq*, a stir-fry of caribou meat and onions. What was once a white coffee maker, now stained brown from countless pots of coffee, began to gurgle with a fresh brew. Jupi took a seat at the kitchen table, turned up the volume on the radio, listened to community members share birthday wishes from all over the territory.

Aatami handed his father a plate of rice and caribou meat, handing him also a can of Pepsi and setting an almost empty bottle of China Lily soya sauce on the table. Jupi took it gratefully, regretting his earlier urge to sigh at the sight of his two sons.

"Your boss has been calling," Mark said, not taking his eyes off the television.

Jupi grunted, "I'll go in tomorrow," as he plowed the food into his mouth. Now that he was home, he could smell the booze on his breath and clothing. He was not ashamed. It was the only way he knew how to cope.

An easy silence followed, with just the sounds of the radio and quiet chants when one of the hockey teams made a goal or the other team got a penalty.

As he took his first sips of coffee, Jupi said to the room, "Next time I go on my long hunting trip, I need one of you to come with me."

Mark and Aatami reluctantly looked at their father. Jupi could see them both trying to calculate a response.

Jupi knew what was going through their heads. They went hunting with their father often enough when they were able to pay for their share of gas and bullets. But the long hunting trip had always been a solitary event for their father, where he'd come back with no catch, stinking of whatever alcohol he could get his hands on.

"Sure, *Ataat*," Mark said, always ready to please. Aatami remained quiet, always a man of few words.

"Next trip will be in April," Jupi said.

Upirngassaaq | Early Spring

III.

By the time April rolled around, Aatami was in jail after a bad bender fraught with petty crimes. Mark tagged along on the "long hunting trip," but could only make it halfway to the site of the qulliq before he refused to go any further.

"This is fucked up." Mark's tone was bereft of its usual nonchalance. He took deep, uncomfortable breaths, but Jupi didn't think it was because the hike was tiring and difficult. He could see Mark's obvious distress.

Jupi asked him to keep it together, "Come on, it's not too much further. I need you to join me."

"No fucking way." Mark turned back.

Jupi darted to grab his arm, but Mark wrung it away with such aggression that they both slipped and toppled over into the snow.

"Can't you feel it?" Mark's voice was strangled between the urge to yell and hiss as he struggled to get back onto his feet. "Can't you *hear* them? We shouldn't be here. We shouldn't fucking be here!"

Jupi tried to stand back up. Mark, noticing his father's movement, lunged to pin him to the ground. Overwhelmed by Mark's frantic behaviour, Jupi struggled to figure out what to say. He had always thought of his middle son as too erratic for the meetings with Kipik. He had never been able to read how Mark would react to any given situation.

"Son," Jupi managed to say, using all his strength to push against Mark's weight. "This is important, we need to—"

But Mark stood and ran unsteadily through the deep snow, ignoring Jupi's attempts to call him back. Eventually the drone of a Ski-Doo started up and Jupi could hear Mark drive off, back the way they came.

Alone, Jupi continued forward. The fire needed to be lit.

He waited for several hours, until he felt the chill down to his bones, but Kipik did not show up in the end.

Jupi was not surprised. He never knew exactly when the spirit would return. Though he could usually count on seeing the spirit at least once a year, the longest he'd gone without seeing Kipik was after Jupi's father had passed away. It had been five years between Kipik's visits that time, so long that Jupi considered quitting the duty of the long hunting trip altogether.

Two years passed before Jupi saw Kipik again. This time, there was no exchange of pleasantries. Kipik was not one to beat around the bush.

"Still no sons with you." Kipik seemed to materialize their vocal chords before everything else, their hoarse voice settling quickly into multiple tenors, a creature of a thousand voices, using them all at once. "I warned you last time."

"My sons . . . they are not fit to meet you, Kipik. They would go mad if I brought them here," Jupi confessed.

The spirit recoiled in anger, their shape became less discernible, their voices booming, "What provokes you to insult me so?"

Jupi looked away, unable to face the disturbing image of the spirit. "*Ilaa*, it's just—" He drew a heavy breath, facing the reality of what his sons had become. He'd ignored it for years, unable to face the responsibility of how and why they'd turned out the way they had. Jupi sighed and, through a lump in his throat, carried on. "My boys are alcoholics and drug addicts, mentally ill. My oldest son is dead and my youngest is in jail."

Kipik's shape solidified. Curious, they waited for the old hunter to continue.

Jupi shook his head in thought. "Those of us who were born in the old times, still in tents and *qarmaqs*, we went through so many changes. Hard things to go through. But we came out strong. Tough. My sons? I provided them with everything I could, and they didn't come out strong like me. I couldn't protect my children. They—*aamai*—they just aren't like me. I've tried to teach them the old ways, but they've never been stable enough."

"You failed them?" Kipik's tone was full of accusation.

"No, they've always been soft. Sensitive," Jupi justified.

"You failed them." A statement.

"How?" Jupi asked, and there was genuine desperation in the question. Not in defense, as it had been only a moment before, but in relief of a long-buried feeling. "How have I failed them? I raised them how I was raised. I wasn't perfect, but neither was my father."

"That's what you have all always said. Raising children how you were raised, not perfect but neither were your parents." Kipik's booming voices had receded, calming back into those ancient vocal cords. "But you all never take responsibility for the times that you weren't perfect, for the times where you hurt your children."

"How are we supposed to know better?" Again, Jupi's question was genuine, not defensive.

"It is not that you are supposed to know better." Kipik did not elaborate.

A silence.

"Help me," Jupi pled.

"I have already helped you," Kipik replied. "Tell me your stories, then we will be on our way. Next time, bring me a successor."

Jupi, ever the faithful servant, proceeded to tell Kipik his stories.

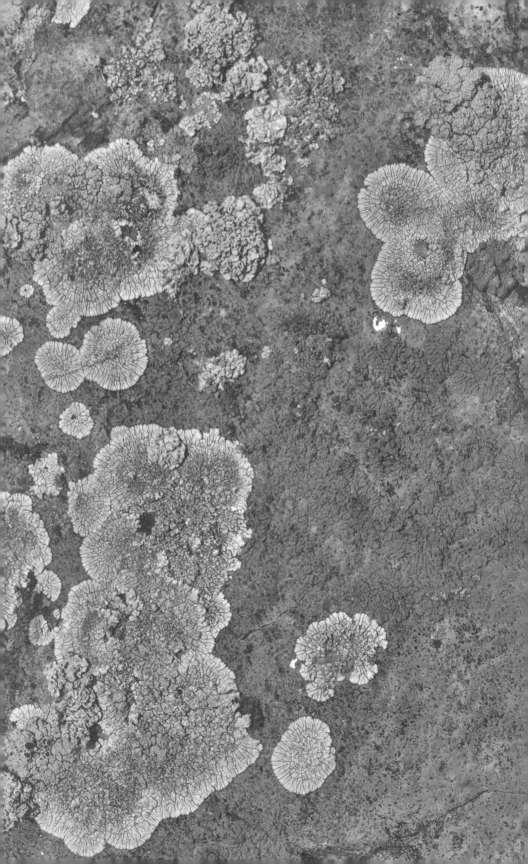

Tarnikuluk

Tulugaq stood on the sturdy telephone pole in front of a church in the community. To the people gathering at the small building, he only appeared as a raven observing the view. It seemed as if the whole community had come to the church today, as they were overflowing out of the structure, spilling onto the street. There was a mess of vehicles parked—pick-up trucks, small SUVs, and dozens of snowmobiles. Weepy singing lilted out of the church as the people sang their sorrows. A death had come to the community again, and this was the funeral for yet another young soul who tripped into the idea that dying by one's own hand might make their sadness end.

Another soul joined Tulugaq on the telephone pole in the form of a smaller, less majestic raven. She was shy and hesitant, confused at why there were so many people below them. Tulugaq waited for her to gain enough courage to speak. Several moments later, in a squawk, she asked, "Is that my funeral?"

He nodded his head in assent and looked at Little Soul, so crumpled and quiet. In her life, she did not often know happiness. Her spirit was a mixture of bland colours that did not convey the potential she had to be a noteworthy person. She had let these colours overbear her, hiding the truth of her essence: magenta, turquoise, cobalt, and gold. She stared at the crowd for a long time, eventually asking, "Why are there so many?"

"Your death has devastated the community," Tulugaq shared without needing anymore prompting. He was here to guide her, not to make her feel worse. "As all deaths do. However, the death of a soul so young and vulnerable creates such a tear in the fabric of the town. They are all thinking of their own shortcomings in helping you when you were alive. They are remembering the times they saw you, knowing that you needed help, and they did nothing."

A silence followed as Little Soul contemplated this, taking in the meaning of what Tulugaq had detailed.

As the mournful sounds below them grew louder, more frightened and upset, they bore witness as a closed, basic wooden casket was carried out by six uniformed cadets. Little Soul remembered that she had been a cadet, too, but she had stopped going the year before. Her fellow cadets carried the wooden box and gently laid it in the bed of a pick-up truck. She could see their glistening cheeks, wet with tears, from the top of the telephone pole.

Alive, she hadn't been very close to any of them. In fact, in her final months of life, she hadn't been close to anyone. Her family was in shambles, in a constant strain against addiction and hunger. Little Soul had found refuge with cousins and friends, but she always felt that she had overstayed her welcome and eventually returned home. Many of her relationships had begun to fall apart. Living in poverty, Little Soul had stolen money and little trinkets from her friends and their families, had alienated herself by saying things behind their backs knowing that someone would overhear her. It wasn't something she could control—Little Soul had to lash out. She'd wanted them to hurt as much as she did.

Little Soul sat on the telephone pole, watching the people file out of the building. First, community members, peers from school, teachers, and childhood friends came out with all their sorrowful eyes. Then her relatives from out of town, her cousins, aunts, uncles, siblings, and lastly, her mother. All their grief-stricken faces stung Little Soul, but it was the vacant look in her mother's face that haunted her the most.

Tulugaq noticed Little Soul's trembling at the sight of her family, the denial in her eyes. At first, he assumed she was denying that she was dead. Then, in an unhappy squawk, Little Soul cried, "My mother still doesn't care! Still! How can she be so cruel to me, even now? She always hated me!"

Throughout his immortal life—a fate given to him as punishment for tricking Nuliajuk into marrying him and terrifying her father into drowning her—Tulugaq had guided innumerable souls from their suicides to their next spiritual forms. There was no way to count the number of lonely and anxious souls he'd met. It did not surprise him that Little Soul reacted this way to her mother's seemingly emotionless appearance.

"She is mourning her youngest daughter, Little Soul," Tulugaq cooed. "Everyone processes their grief differently."

"She never loved me!" Little Soul said, ignoring him.

Tulugaq patiently waited for her anger to pass. For several moments, she mourned her life for all its difficulty, all the cruelty she had suffered.

Tulugaq knew of many stories similar to Little Soul's. He'd carried them over, consoled souls as lost as hers, onto the next stage of death.

Every time he heard their stories, Tulugaq shrank. His life's purpose had been about mischief, making himself happy, playing jokes on people and getting the things he wanted. He would use people's overheard secrets as leverage, use his wits to steal whatever he pleased, from beautifully crafted ivory snow knives to gorgeous women. He'd misjudged the situation with Nuliajuk. Ever since she became a powerful sea spirit through his malice, the mother of sea mammals, Tulugaq couldn't stop thinking about how petty he had been. He'd started out as a vibrant celestial being. Now, he couldn't grow any larger than the raven form he took.

Each time the souls came, Tulugaq dimmed.

Their lives carried such darkness and apathy. Lives lived on a constant edge, inching closer to the abyss each and every moment that someone sneered at them, raised a hand to them, every time they felt lonely or foolish. Until one day someone just said one word, any single word, and suddenly it all tumbled down on top of them. They lost their footing on that cliff's edge, and they couldn't remember the things that had kept them together for so long. Tulugaq swallowed their painful lives in order to bring them to their next spiritual life in a way that would rid them of their terrible sadness, but doing this meant that he soaked it all up. He became more and more tired, more and more remorseful.

Year after year, the number of souls multiplied as a mental health crisis ravaged the communities. Colonial traumas systemically cycled through the generations. There was no support in the communities, everyone vicariously inheriting more traumas, everyone burning out.

Still, Tulugaq had to help Little Soul see that she must move on.

"Little one," Tulugaq spoke, his eons of life resounding through his voice, "You must see. You will never be truly happy, in no matter which form of life, whether human or spiritual, you will never be fully satisfied. You have closed yourself off from that possibility."

"You don't know!" Little Soul wept. "You don't understand what it was like. You don't know how I lived!"

Yes, Little Soul, I do, he thought quietly to himself. I know how the forty-year-old man felt last week, after his wife of twenty years left him. I know how the sixteen-year-old girl felt a month ago. I know how the thirteen-year-old boy felt four years ago. I know how the eleven-year-old felt. I know how you felt.

"I do, little one." He inclined his head toward her, brushing away his heavy thoughts. "You have let your sadness and your obstacles become you. Until you break free from those, I cannot help."

Little Soul whimpered. Below, the crowd had dispersed. The family had gone with her body off to the cemetery at the edge of town, whilst her old friends and other members of the community made their way home. Stores, office buildings, and schools were temporarily closed for the service. Her old classmates and teachers would all be returning to classes tomorrow.

Tulugaq could feel her vulnerability, her undiluted hopelessness. He hopped closer to her and listened while she breathed heavily between her sobs. Why, she wondered, why was everyone around her so much stronger while she was too weak to even hold herself up?

"I am here," Tulugaq continued to explain, "so that I may help you carry onward and learn to accept yourself for who you are, and to understand that you didn't deserve any of the circumstances that made your life hard, to accept that those who had hurt you were only suffering, too.

"When you accept yourself and your life, you accept all the harshness, but also the joy. When you accept these things, you may move on. You can dance in the stars or swim in the ocean. Your acceptance of yourself is what will free you. Your acceptance of your circumstances is your deliverance. This will be very hard, indeed. It will also be truly rewarding."

"But I don't care about me," Little Soul murmured. "I mean, yes, I do . . . but I could accept myself just fine. I just can't . . . I can't accept them. My mother, my father, the bullies. I can't do that. They hurt me too much."

"I understand," Tulugaq said. "And you do not need to forgive them. But you must come to a point where you can accept what happened to you and move on."

She retreated to her silence.

Tulugaq continued, "I've done wrong, little one. I've done such terrible wrong to others, none of whom have forgiven me. For millennia, those I hurt have punished me, making me pay my due for the pain I've caused them. They have not forgiven me, and though I am suffering, I forgive them. I deserved this punishment, and they do not feel that I have redeemed myself."

"You think I should forgive my mother?" Little Soul scorned. "My father? My bullies and the others who were mean to me? You think they deserve it? Just like you think you deserve the forgiveness of the one's you've hurt?"

"I think everyone deserves redemption and forgiveness. It heals those who are unhealthy, mends those who are broken. You know . . . some of those people that went to your funeral are angry at you. They think you are selfish and cowardly. They think you left them behind, that you took yourself from them. You were important in their lives and you took yourself away, from them and from future generations. Yet, they forgive you, because they cared for you. I think you deserve forgiveness. I think your mother deserves forgiveness, and all the others in your life. People aren't born evil, they are moulded. Your mother suffered long and hard as a child. She doesn't know how else to live."

Silence again. It wore on for a string of time that none could measure, lasting both a minute and a century. They sat comfortably, even with the thick tension between their hunched shoulders.

Finally, Little Soul spoke, her voice carrying graceful strength, "Okay."

"You forgive?" he prompted.

"I forgive them," she spoke gently into the wind. "I forgive them all: those that you have wronged, you for hurting them, my family, my mother, my friends." She looked over the town, cloaked in white snow, puffs of smoke wafting from chimneys, growling engines of snowmobiles riling in the distance. Little Soul took a deep breath, saying, "I forgive myself."

As she flew away, light bearing upon her soul, taking her to new places, new life, Tulugaq remembered that at least one of those he had wronged had forgiven him. Nuliajuk may have given him this job as punishment, but she also knew how rewarding it felt to send a passing soul soaring into the sunlight.

If you or someone you know may be contemplating suicide, please access the resources below for support:

Nunavut Kamatsiaqtut Helpline (English and Inuktitut): 1-867-979-3333 or 1-800-265-3333 (24/7)

Kids Help Phone (English): Use the online chat at kidshelpphone.ca, call 1-800-668-6868, or text CONNECT to 686868 (24/7)

The LifeLine App: Provides call, text, and online chat services (24/7)

Crisis Services Canada (English): Use the online chat at 988.ca, or call or text 988 (24/7)

Your local Health Centre

IV.

"That will do." Though Kipik said this, their tone suggested otherwise. This story did not do. Too much had transpired beforehand. Both hunter and spirit were unconvinced and unenthused.

"I will not wait so long to see you again," Kipik continued. "The next solstice, I will be here. If you do not have a successor by then, do not bother to show up. This is your only duty."

"But my sons—"

Kipik's form raised a hand-like limb. "If you do not think your sons are worthy of me, then you must find someone else. They must have your blood. On them or within them, that is all I need. You do remember why I need your blood, yes?"

Jupi nodded.

"Next solstice." Kipik's final warning.

"Next solstice." Jupi agreed.

With that, Kipik receded into the foundation of the cliffside. Always fading into a trick of the light, a ray of sunlight bursting and obscuring their disappearance.

As always, Jupi waited for a time, then he extinguished the flame before making the journey back to the Ski-Doo. This time, he did not linger at his cabin, he only stopped there to eat a bit of food and refill his gas tank, then he returned home.

He spent weeks trying to convince Mark to come back to the cliffside with him, to no avail. Mark had barely recovered from the last trip and had gone on a long bender before he'd finally sought treatment in southern Canada. He'd only returned recently, and he avoided his father at almost any cost.

Aatami, too, was due to arrive in June, but the risk was too high for Jupi to bank on Aatami being his successor. What if Aatami had an incident in the jail that resulted in him staying longer? What if the justice system just failed to release him in time? What if it worked out and Aatami was able to come, but Kipik was offended by Aatami's presence and destroyed them both?

Jupi sought his nephews, his cousins, any boy who was remotely related to him, but none had the quality that Jupi knew Kipik needed. Kipik had said that it was only blood, but Jupi knew better.

Jupi's successor needed an open mind and heart, and most important of all, they needed to be a storyteller. They needed to be able to balance stories the way Inuit legends always have; full of darkness and terror, but often with the protagonist outwitting their adversary.

From the moment Inuit can stand on their own two feet, they are taught to think for the good of the family and the community, to be respectful, and to be clever in many capacities.

Think outside the box, don't dwell on the sad or hard things, crack a good joke, be resourceful, and outwit the spirits.

For generations, Jupi and his ancestors were raised to be storytellers, specifically for Kipik. An old promise made by a grandfather many times removed, an ancestor who'd done something to garner the attention of a spirit, leaving an oath to be repaid.

Over millennia, the stories were not always true. They were sometimes created in the hopes of lightening the burden of hardship, to brighten the unending darkness of winter, and sometimes they were created on a whim in the glory of high summer, when the sun moved in a circle throughout the sky, dipping low, but never so low as to graze the horizon at all.

How could a spirit know that this was not a common trait among the people? Especially now, after Inuit lives had changed so drastically in only one generation. And as each new generation came, the more their culture and traditions changed.

No, Jupi would not allow this role to die with him. He would not fail his ancestor, a hundred grandfathers ago. Jupi would pass on the burden, but only to one who was strong enough to bear the weight.

Endlessly, he asked his family, even seeking those in other communities and offering to either drive his Ski-Doo over the hundreds of kilometres to pick them up or pay for their flights. He had no luck.

Upirngaaq | Spring

V.

This was the first time that Kipik had confirmed they would be there at the next solstice. Jupi refused to take that warning lightly.

When Aatami finally returned home, however, Jupi was deflated further. It was evident that his youngest son could not succeed him. Though he was stable enough now, there was too much still buried within him still needing to be healed. If he were to come with Jupi, Kipik would break Aatami piece by piece without uttering a word, without lifting a tendril.

But Aatami's return was not fruitless. Returning with him was his long-time on-and-off girlfriend, and their ten-year-old precocious daughter.

"Let me take her on my long hunting trip," Jupi begged. He made sure to do so when Mark was out of town, off to his rotation of work at the iron ore mine further north. "She's grown up away from here, she needs to connect with the land."

Aatami was hesitant. He'd only had her back in his life for a few months. "Maati is so sensitive, Ataat," he argued. "She only speaks *Qallunaatitut*, and you only speak Inuktitut. She doesn't even know you. She hardly knows me."

"I speak English at work. But anyways, that's what makes it more important." Jupi could not hide his desperation, the solstice was only a week away, "Please, Irniapik. You can come, too, if you'd like, but I can only take you as far as the cabin. From there, Maati and I must go on the path alone, like my father and I did, and he and his father did before."

"Why not me?" Aatami's voice was choked around a lump. There was both an adult resolve and childlike insecurity. "Why can't you take me?"

Jupi had come to terms with this, after Kipik's admonishment. No longer hiding from the truth, Jupi said, "Because I failed you, Irniapik. I made you settle for the life I had, instead of providing you with something better. I gave you scraps instead of the best possibilities. Now I must do better for your *panik*. Please, son. If I cannot bring her, then everything is lost."

The next week, Jupi and Maati were navigating a melting terrain, having left Aatami at the cabin. Maati clung to her grandfather. She had grown up mostly in the south as her mother attended university. Her only experience was the rare summer visits back home, where Jupi often only saw her once or twice.

Maati had complained the whole way to the cabin, had begged not to come on the long hunting trip alone with her grandfather, had cried while she clung to her grandfather on the snowmobile, but as soon as he turned off the engine, her whole demeanor changed. She quieted, narrowed her eyes in the exact direction of the inlet.

Jupi removed the rifle that was slung across his chest, double checked the safety, then leaned it against his machine. He removed his parka. He was wearing his bib-style snow pants over a wool sweater that his late wife had knitted for him twenty years ago. He untied his pack from the back of his snowmobile, pulling out a light down-filled puffer coat. He urged Maati to do the same, and she removed her parka and put the new coat on, then watched as her grandfather tied down their parkas to the machine in the place where his pack had been. He slung the backpack over his shoulders, grabbed his rifle, and hung it over his shoulder.

"Come on," he said, his Inuk accent thick as he spoke English for the first time in years. "It's a hard walk."

"Where are we?" Maati asked.

"*Atiqaqquujingimmat*, I don't think this place have a name," Jupi explained, struggling through the grammar of another language. "No one knows about it. Only me."

"Why?" Maati asked, and in a quick breath, added, "And it's 'has a name,' not 'have a name.'"

"Ermmm . . . " Jupi trekked forward, the path already becoming difficult. "It is a place connected to our family. To my great-great-great-great-great-great grampa or something. Maybe there's more great-great-great-greats. We've been coming here for hundreds of years."

"Why?" Maati repeated.

"You'll see," Jupi replied.

"Just tell me," Maati said matter-of-factly, shedding the whiny tone she'd had all day and transforming instead to that of impatience.

"It's just easier to show you," Jupi told her.

Her questions continued, but she kept pace as a strange fascination overcame her. As they reached the point where Mark had turned back, Jupi stopped for a moment and looked at her. Maati's cheeks were bright red with the exertion from the hike, but her eyes were wide, taking in everything about the place. Instead of soft snow, they were trekking through slush, but neither complained.

"You okay?" Jupi asked.

"Mhmm," she replied.

They continued until they reached their inlet, the snowmelt revealing the rocky beach littered with shells and skeletons of small animals. Jupi told her to sit and watch him as he started his work. After all the decades of coming here, it had become a ritual. "You watch me, okay? That's how Inuit learn. By watching."

He laid his backpack on the ground, took off his rifle and leaned it safely against a rock, then he kneeled at the edge of a round hearth of rocks. He swept aside a layer of slushy snow to reveal an almond-shaped stone lamp nestled in the centre of the hearth. He produced a piece of driftwood with a burnt tip, and two sealed bags from his backpack. Inside the first was a slab of seal fat, wrapped up in several layers of plastic bags to prevent the grease from seeping onto the fabric. In the other was a combination of Arctic cotton and peat moss, shredded together to make a wick for the stone lamp.

"You know what this is?" Jupi asked his granddaughter.

She shrugged. "Kind of. It's a koolick, right?"

"Eee, what did they even teach you at Ottawa?" he asked her. Maati did not reply. Jupi corrected her pronunciation, "It's *qulliq*."

Maati, unpracticed in actually speaking Inuktitut and not having the right muscles in her throat, tried again, "kool-lick."

"*Aaka*," Jupi corrected. "Qud-liq."

She produced an exaggerated sound from the back of her throat as she tried to mimic her grandfather's pronunciation. "Qqqqoooo-liqqqqq," Maati attempted again.

"Qud-liq." He tried again.

"QQQQOO—"

"Okay, that's enough." Jupi shook his head, but he found himself smiling, chuckling softly. He laid a small chunk the seal fat onto the qulliq and took out a small mallet. He started to hammer at the seal fat until it was pounded into a thin liquid layer. Then he took some of the wick mixture, dabbed it a bit into the seal fat, and laid it on the lip of the lamp. With a lighter, he lit the edge of the wick and nurtured the flame with the piece of driftwood he'd taken out of his bag earlier. Soon, a line of flame was steadily lit, six perfect triangles across the qulliq lip.

The inlet, though difficult to get to, was almost an oasis in the middle of a treacherous area. The wind did not reach the qulliq flame, and the sun beat down.

A soft silence followed the lighting of the qulliq.

"Now what?" Maati asked after a while.

"We're waiting for my friend," Jupi answered.

The wait ended up being so long that Jupi was afraid Kipik would not show up. Maati grew more impatient, wandering around the little site, picking up the skeletons of lemmings that the birds had left over the years. When she finally settled back to sit, the trick of the light came, and Kipik emerged.

Maati gasped, but otherwise remained silent.

Jupi, his father, and grandfathers before him had never brought a girl to Kipik. Jupi had been willing to live with the consequences if her presence offended the spirit, but still, he held his breath.

Kipik's eyes were always the first part to form when the spirit took shape. They looked at Jupi briefly before settling on

Maati. There was a twinkle in the spirit's gaze, their vertical mouth settled into a grin.

"Jupi," Kipik spoke.

"Kipik," Jupi replied.

Kipik's eyes did not waver from the little girl. The spirit waited.

The little girl sat rigidly, entranced and unable to tear her eyes away from the presence of Kipik. She was scarcely breathing.

"This is my granddaughter," Jupi said. "Maati."

"A successor," Kipik replied, "*finally*."

Maati remained silent, sat unmoving with a straight back.

Kipik, still staring, demanded, "Maati, tell me a story."

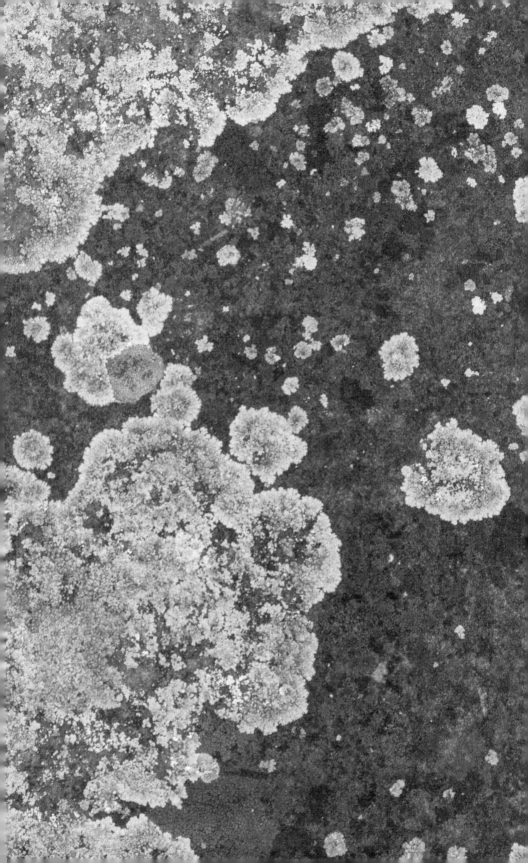

Welcome to Maktaaq City

A cry can be heard across the tundra. A hesitant cry at first, as though the one who put it into the world wasn't sure it had the power to make such a sound. Then, as they hear their cry span out, as they gain their footing, their next wail is unleashed with the full knowledge of their lungs' capacity.

A young woman, on her knees, hunched over on a hillside not too far away, perks up. She looks away from her berry-picking patch, putting the few berries that were in her hands into the bucket at her side. The woman has just heard the cry of a newborn baby. She almost feels like rolling her eyes, but she calls out, "*Tusaaviuk*? Do you hear it?"

Another woman, also in the same position not too far away, sighs. She looks in the direction the cry has come from. She replies with an annoyed, "Yup."

They stand up from their kneeling positions, stretch, and begin walking. They follow the sound of the baby's crying. It is only a short walk, both following their gut instinct that the cries are coming from a patch of soft earth surrounded by the sweet pink flowers of summer. *Paunnait*, dwarf fireweed.

The cries become desperate, filled with the baby's need for skin-to-skin contact, for a soothing voice, for milk.

As they reach the patch, they hear the baby's cries from a small opening in the ground that looks like it could be the entry to a small animal's burrow. The first woman, Putuguq, kneels and reaches into the burrow. She pulls the baby out from the ground's womb. The baby is covered in dirt, but their cries instantly silence. She asks the other, "Am I cursed or something?"

The other woman, Ida, shrugs. "Seems like it's only you who finds them."

"*Angakkuuvungaqai*?" Putuguq says. "Maybe I'm a shaman?"

The women are quiet for a moment in deep thought, then they snort with laughter. Putuguq adds, "Ah, I really hope not."

They look at the baby she holds in her arms. The infant is naked, but does not seem to feel cold nor warmth. Ida takes off her green, floral granny-scarf and lays it on the ground. Putuguq puts the baby atop, wipes the dirt away with her sleeve, then swaddles the baby into Ida's scarf. Once they are bundled up, she holds the baby against her chest, gently rocking her body up and down to keep the baby calm.

"Ugly baby," says Ida.

"Don't say such things," Putuguq chides. "We all come into this world ugly."

"Mmmm," mutters Ida. "But not all of us stay ugly like you."

"Shut up," Putuguq smacks Ida's arm, but a smile finds itself on her lips.

"Atii," Ida says. "Let's go home. We need to bring the baby to Denis."

Denis is not a person, but a colloquial term for the Department of Nunamiinngaaqtut Services (DNS). It is a haphazard department created in the last few years as more infants are being found out on the land. It works, more or less, as an orphanage.

It is their second or third time finding a *Nunamiinngaaqtut*, a child born from the earth, in the last few weeks, and they have come prepared. Ida takes out a bottle of formula milk and gives it to Putuguq to feed the baby. She also takes out a homemade vest with a big pouch in the back, a modern-summertime-zip-up-*amauti*, and she holds it out to show Putuguq, prompting her to wear it.

Putuguq, whose hands are full, asks, "Can't you carry the baby this time?"

"Yuck." Ida doesn't care much for babies and would rather not carry them on her back. "That's for mothers, not berry-pickers."

"I'm just a berry-picker, too, you know," Putuguq replies, but she lets Ida put the amauti around her, putting Putuguq's arms through the holes one at a time, and zipping it up in the back. Now the baby can lay against her chest and Putuguq's hands can be free.

"Look at it this way," Ida says, "now I have to carry all our bags and berries back into town."

Putuguq narrows her eyes, sucking air through her teeth, "Cchhh! You just have to carry them to the Honda."

Ida smiles, "What can I say, Put. Sucks to be you, man."

Putuguq slaps Ida's arm again, but they are burdened by laughter. They make their way from the berry-picking area and back to the road. Ida puts lids onto the buckets full of berries and sets them into two milk crates bungeed on the front rack of their ATV. She starts the machine, and Putuguq sits on the back, one hand braced on the baby laying on her chest, the fingers of her other hand clinging to the metal rack for safety.

Once they roll back into town, passing by the airport, the jail, the garages, then the government buildings, the grocery store, the elementary school, and the Elder's centre, they turn down a road toward the beach. It isn't the smartest place to have an orphanage, considering the creatures that live near ice floes and the shoreline, but there were no other buildings available at the time Denis was created.

Inside Denis, there is already a line formed. It appears that two others have found babies today. The babies they hold are silent, just as the one Putuguq and Ida have found has been silent since being picked up.

Nunamiinngaaqtuit don't like making a fuss. Their purpose is supposed to bring joy to a community in need after great loss, but lately there is no joy at the sight of the babies from the earth. Too many children are going missing, always followed by the birth of a Nunamiinngaaqtut.

Mattaaq City is overpopulated enough as it is, with all the *qallupilluit* (sea creatures who steal babies), *ijirait* (evil beings who steal *and* eat babies, probably), *kajjait* (cursed wolves who are always hungry and probably also eat babies), *inukpasugjuit* (giants . . . no information on their stance on eating babies), and—worst of all—transient *qallunaat* (white people . . . who definitely steal babies). According to legends, Nunamiinngaaqtuit were supposed to be born to couples who could not have children of their own, or after times of famine to help repopulate.

They have no place here and now. Life is not as it once was, where each day required an outrageous amount of work to prepare for the next, to ensure that life carried on. Now, there are luxuries like houses, and rifles, and grocery stores, and money.

Finally, Putuguq, Ida, and the baby reach the front of the line and are greeted by a woman covered in traditional tattoos on her face, hands, and arms. She looks at the baby, then up at the women. She rolls her eyes, putting her fingers to her temples, and sighs. "Another one, Putuguq?"

Putuguq raises her eyebrows in confirmation and echoes her earlier musing, "Angakkuqpungaqai?"

The tattooed woman sees no humour in Putuguq's words. She takes her fingers away from her temples and grabs a pen. Matter-of-factly, she says, "If you think that you may be a shaman, I would encourage you to take the *Angakkuq* Aptitude Tests at the Arctic College. There is a $25 fee."

Putuguq smiles wanly and hands the baby over to Ida. "Just kidding, sorry."

The tattooed woman hands a form and the pen over to Putuguq. Having done this twice already, Putuguq is able to get through the form quickly. She hands it back and waits for the tattooed woman to look it over. Once that is done, the tattooed woman reaches her arms out and Ida hands the baby over.

"That's my scarf," Ida informs her in a tip-toeing voice.

"Great, I'll consider it a donation then," replies the tattooed woman. Then she gives them a pointed look and gestures to the exit. "Bye!"

Putuguq and Ida leave in haste.

The tattooed woman observes the baby for a moment. She furrows her brow, hands the baby over to another employee, who hands them over to another, and yet another, until finally they are given to a motherly woman to be fed, then put into a proper nursery bed.

After a while, the staff at Denis decide to name them Paunnaq. They hope Paunnaq will end up okay.

"I mean," says one of the staff, "the mayor of Maktaaq City is Nunamiinngaaqtut herself, so this one could do great things, too. I think."

They have high hopes for Paunnaq and all other Nunamiinngaqtuit in their care.

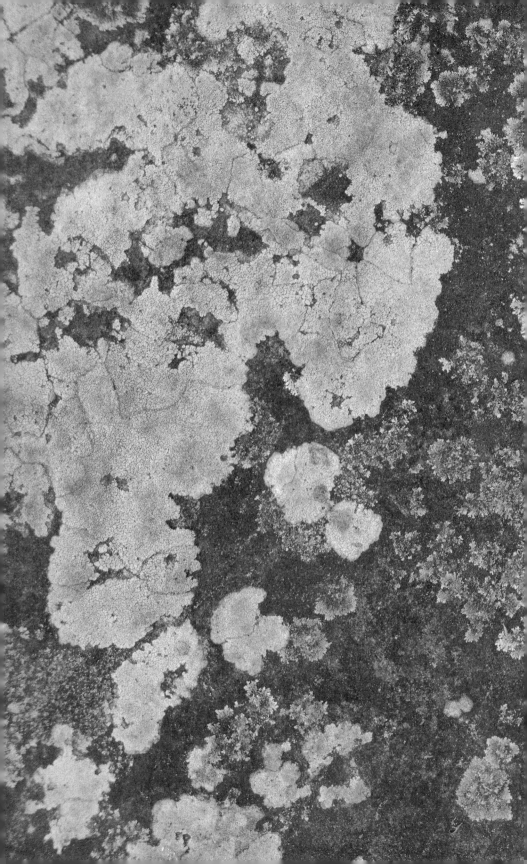

VI.

Jupi could feel the sweat dripping down his spine, a ribbon of relief flooding through him. Maati had performed a hundred times better than he could have dreamed.

Kipik seemed to be feeling the same. The spirit's vertical mouth was grinning as wide as can be, a disgusting gash of sharp teeth. For a moment, neither Jupi nor Kipik said anything. Maati sat patiently, swinging her little legs as she waited for more instructions, for feedback, for what would happen next.

Jupi coughed, wiped his face as he realized tears had welled in his eyes. He was taught never to be proud, there is always room for improvement and work to be done. But the surge of pride he felt for his granddaughter, who he hardly knew, overwhelmed him.

Perhaps she was so great because she had grown up so far from him.

Kipik's voices rose in a cacophony, *"Finally.* You are who we have been waiting for."

Maati still did not speak. Her legs still swung.

"You must come every season, for every lighting of the qulliq," Kipik commanded. "You must learn to read the seasons, to understand the moon's path. You must take this mantle over from your grandfather."

Maati nodded, and though she did not grow up consistently around Inuktitut, she seemed to understand everything Kipik said, despite the spirit speaking an old, traditional dialect. It was the same for Kipik, because Maati had told her story in English, and the spirit had understood.

"Was it good?" Maati asked.

"Very," Kipik said. "You are much more talented than your grandfather."

One of the spirit's vertical eyes winked, the impression of a laugh sounding from their mouth.

Maati blushed, averted her gaze downward. Sheepishly, she glanced toward Jupi, then back to her feet.

"Until next time," Kipik said, and—in a flash—vanished.

As they hiked back, Maati did not speak. The pride Jupi had felt began to morph into something more uncomfortable. He was worried. Would she ever speak again?

Once they made it back to the snowmobiles, Jupi told her to change back into her parka. She did as she was told, and as she switched from her light, down-filled coat to her baby blue pullover parka, he could see that she was trembling. When her head poked out of her hood, he could see she was crying.

She went limp in his arms when he embraced her, and she sobbed into his chest.

He realized, then, that this was the first time he hardly felt any of the tremors he usually did after his meetings with Kipik. It made sense to Jupi, now that Maati was overcome with an onslaught of feelings.

"What was that?" she cried.

"It was a spirit; ancient thing." Jupi told her. "I don't know what happened, but one of our ancestors made a deal with the spirit and we have to come here five times a year to tell stories."

"Why?" Maati's questions echoed those she'd had earlier in the day, but now they were distraught instead of curious.

"I don't know why." Jupi tried his best to comfort her, the warmth coming much easier for her than it had for his sons. "Will you be okay?"

"I'm okay," she said, her heaving breaths finally slowing.

"You were really great," Jupi praised her. "I'm happy you came with me."

"Is it always like that?" Maati asked. "Scary?"

"Were you scared?" Jupi asked her, and he half bent down to get a good look at her face.

She looked back at him. "Big time."

"You didn't even show it," Jupi told her, a smile spreading over his face. "You were very brave."

"Like you?" She buried her face into the white fox fur on the rim of her hood, hiding her face.

"I'm not brave." Jupi scrunched his face up as his way of disagreeing.

"*Ataata* always tells me that you're very strong and brave," she said quietly. "That you go hunting polar bears alone all the time, and you save the world all the time."

"I think these stories are, um, *qanuai*, not true or something," Jupi said as he patted her back. "Like Super Shamou or something."

"What's Super Shamou?" Maati asked.

"Oh my god, you don't even know who Super Shamou is? What did they teach you at Ottawa?"

"It's '*in* Ottawa'," Maati laughed. "And just tell me."

"Super Shamou is an Inuk superhero, like superman, but he wears rubber boots . . . '*Tuktumi takuvit tappaani? Tappaani?!*'" He imitated the superhero's catchphrase. "*Do you see a caribou up there? Up there?*"

Maati kept laughing all the way to the cabin. When she saw her father, she did not tell him about what had happened, she only talked to him about the Inuk superhero that was her grandfather, *Ittuq* Jupi.

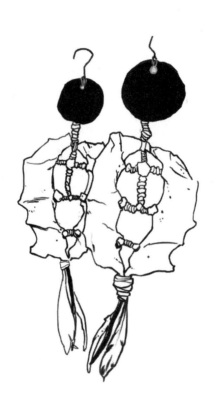

Aujaq | Summer

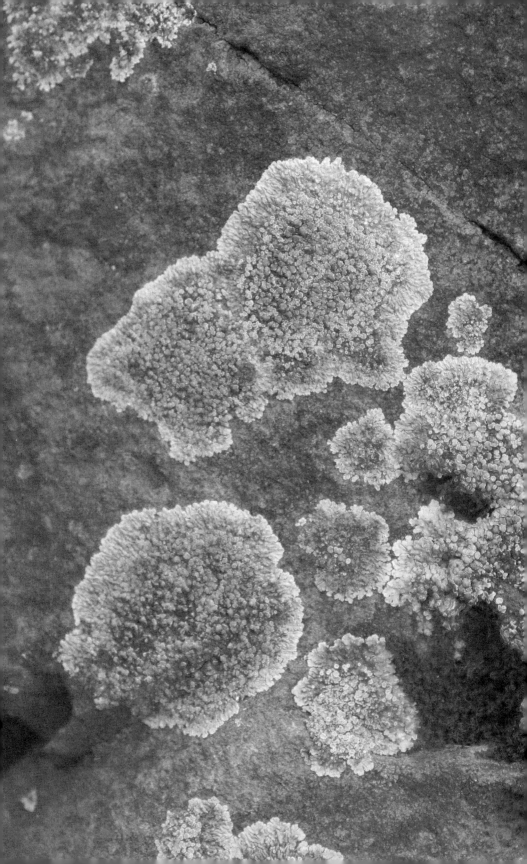

VII.

Jupi's life changed as his relationship with Maati bloomed. They became almost inseparable as he taught her the duties of her new role as his successor. He taught her to hunt as though the land was an extension of her body, until she could read the weather patterns as easily as she could count to ten.

Stories came easily to Maati; she had grown up glued to television, and video games, and books. She grew up with her mother's university classmates, learning the folklore of different Indigenous groups across the south. Whenever she could get her hands on it, Maati's mother would give her books by Inuit authors, rented and purchased movies made by Inuit filmmakers, whether from Nunavut, Nunavik, NWT, Alaska, or Greenland. They hadn't been able to afford trips back home very often, but people always visited, or she and her mom would go visit people at Baffin Larga, the boarding home for Inuit who had to travel to Ottawa for medical reasons. Whenever Tunngasuvingat Inuit, the Inuit association in Ottawa, held community events like feasts and spring celebrations with Inuit performers, they would attend. She was lucky to have so many other Inuit around.

Maati had loved consuming all of it. Her favourite movie for a long time was *Atanarjuat: The Fast Runner*. She'd watched it as a kid and covered her eyes during the vivid sex scene, laughed sheepishly at the scene of the naked man running on the ice, or when one of the bad guys fell over while they were sneaking up on the two brothers sleeping in their caribou-hide tent. It was a graphic movie full of spirituality, violence, and folklore, all in Inuktitut. Maati couldn't understand what was being said, and for a time, she was too slow at reading the subtitles, only understanding less than half of what was being said. Her mother translated parts of it for her, but Maati grew to understand most of it through vibes.

Now that Maati was immersed in her community, she picked up on cultural customs quickly, like respecting and helping Elders whenever she had the opportunity, giving away some of a hunted catch to a beloved family member or namesake or to someone in need, or by observing someone who was teaching her something before bombarding them with questions. She picked up the slang among her peers, becoming almost fluent in Inuktitut within months, building the muscles and practices of the different sounds and pronunciations needed for the language. At first, she'd been teased for being so *qallunaaq* (so white), but it didn't deter her. She figured it wasn't as offensive as being called a "fuckin' Inuk" like she'd been called in Ottawa.

She made friends, but her favourite person was always her Ittuq Jupi. She often went to his work at the power plant after school, smelling all the fumes and covering her ears from the sounds of the generators. Then she'd jump into his truck and ride home with him.

Her parents weren't together anymore, her dad lived with Ittuq Jupi while her mom had housing through her government job. Her parents didn't hate each other, they had always been friends their whole lives. It's hard not to be when living in a small town. Her biological father could often be found at her mom's house, even hanging out with her stepfather without any animosity.

At first, Maati's mom was against her newfound relationship with her grandpa.

"He's not very stable," Maati overheard her mother saying to her dad one time. "What about all those times he came back from his hunting trips drunk? I worked really hard for Maati not to be exposed to that bullshit."

"He's different with her," her dad replied. "I don't know why. But he really is."

Still, Maati was allowed to go on every 'long hunting trip' with Jupi, as long as Aatami was close by. They lit the qulliq every season, but it was years before they saw Kipik again. Maati and Jupi would sit there waiting, sometimes in comfortable silence, sometimes in uproarious laughter.

It wasn't until the June just after Maati turned fifteen when they met Kipik again. By then, Maati had caught plenty of geese, ptarmigans, and fish, several seals, and one caribou, all with the help of Jupi.

Kipik was happy to see Maati again, though her demeanor had changed at the sight of the spirit. The easygoing nature that she'd learned from imitating her grandpa had stiffened. She had a tight-lipped smile when Kipik formed, her tone becoming clipped as she spoke to them.

Kipik did not seem to notice. The spirit simply asked for a new story. Maati cleared her throat and told one.

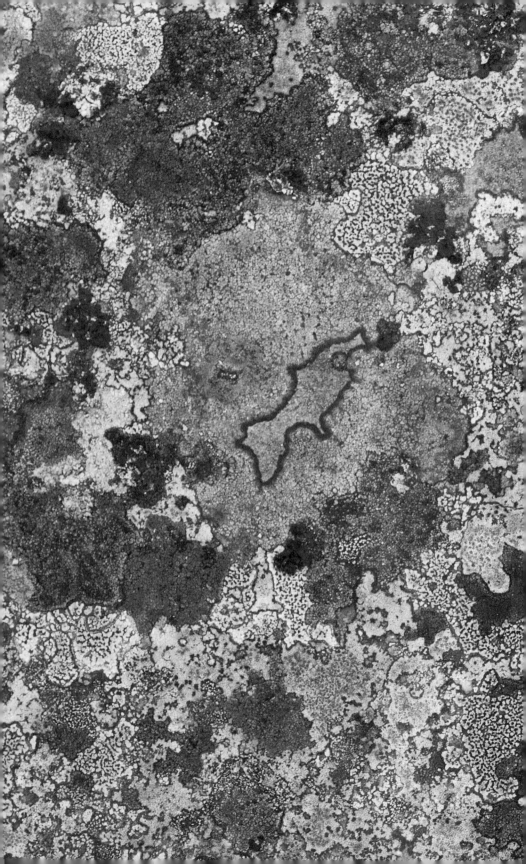

Earring Repair Shop

What goes into the perfect piece of Inuit-made jewellery? Akpa had drawers, shelves, and bins full of all the best materials. Ivory, beads, fox and polar bear fur, sealskin, bowhead whale baleen, beluga vertebrae, narwhal tusk, claws and talons from animals of all sorts, walrus whiskers, caribou antler, ptarmigan feet, muskox horn, soapstone, all worthy specimens in the best of times.

The earring repair shop was nothing more than a shed behind her parent's house. It used to be her father's workshop, where he tinkered with his snowmobile and dried caribou meat and worked on little soapstone carvings to sell for sixty dollars. Enough for a gram of hash. Then he'd take that hash back to the shed and hotknife it with a blowtorch.

But when Akpa's earring repair business started gaining traction and taking up half of the kitchen table, he'd cleaned up the shed for her and taught her how to use the diesel heater. He brought in an old couch and added a twelve-volt outlet and kettle so that Akpa could make French-press coffee. Her mom also helped with fixing up the space, plastering the walls in newspaper to look like the matchbox shacks that were built in the fifties. They brought in repainted cabinetry they'd gotten from various roadsides in town to store her materials. Soon, the shed was not only her workspace, but a place where customers sat around gossiping for hours while she worked.

Akpa didn't mind the gossip. She embraced it, learning all the intricacies of the relationships in town. She knew now that there were certain people to avoid, mostly men who seemed friendly but were actually predators, or girls who tried to fight any person who talked to their boyfriends, or the person who often broke into houses and shacks or went through boats on the beach.

Anything that crossed her table was fair game—beaded necklaces, sterling silver rings with ivory insets, and sealskin bracelets were common enough requests at her shop—but it was earrings that were her specialty. It had all started when a friend asked her to glue the stud back onto a piece of antler; then another friend came asking her to recreate a mirroring sealskin earring after a dog had eaten the other side.

People who had left prospective repairs for weeks that easily morphed into years started showing up when word spread of Akpa fixing so-and-so's earrings. They'd drop off their earrings in the morning or on their lunch break and return after work with something to trade, or with a crisp twenty-dollar bill.

·\ι\ΓΓͰ\ΠΠ·

There was no bell at the door to notify her of someone entering the shack, but there was a gust of cold air. The wind whooshed in, sweeping the little heat that had been cultivated by the heater away. Akpa leaned back in her seat, peering through her workshop doorway. "*Matukauqturuk*!" she exclaimed. "Hurry, close the door!"

Not recognizing the person who had entered, she shut her mouth. Akpa thought that it would be her parents coming in to bring her something to eat. Instead, there was a hooded woman shutting the door against the wind and snow. She wore a luxurious black pullover parka. Silver fox fur trimmed the hood and wrists, and white and gold bias tape and sealskin were intricately detailed throughout. It was one of the most extravagant garments Akpa had ever laid eyes on. Everything about it screamed wealth. The quality of the materials and the skill of the seamstress must have made it cost well over a couple thousand dollars.

The woman shook snow off her shoulders, and her sharp brown eyes darted around the shack.

It was late, Akpa realized. The sun had set long ago in the afternoon and she was sure that her family inside the house were all fast asleep, her parents on the couches with the TV blaring; her brother, his pregnant girlfriend, and their toddler in their bedroom. Akpa hadn't eaten yet. She'd been consumed by beading a necklace back together with a true crime documentary on Netflix playing in the background. She rushed to shut her phone screen off to stop the drone of the documentary's narrator.

When their eyes met, the woman's expression didn't change. Everything about her felt otherworldly, the grace of her neck's movement, the darting of her eyes, the flowing length of her hair. Akpa felt a rush of terror mostly, but also an underlying pang of curiosity. She'd never seen this woman before in her life.

"I—um—I'm closed for the day," Akpa stammered.

An elegant smile spread over the woman's lips, and a voice as smooth as silk slipped out of her mouth. "I know. But I saw the light on."

A shiver spread through Akpa. She had a sense that the woman was trying to come across as humble and comforting, but it was unnatural. She stood from her seat, rubbed her eyes for a moment. She moved past the woman, catching a whiff of burning *qijuktaaq*, Arctic heather, and turned the temperature up on the heater.

The woman seemed unbothered. She walked further inside, staring at the newspaper clippings on the walls. Akpa went to stand by her consultation counter. She coughed, "Ahem—hem—ah—," and an embarrassing wad of phlegm flew out of her throat. Not wanting to spit it out in front of whoever this woman was, Akpa gulped it back down. She coughed once more, then asked, "Uh—what—what can I help you with?"

The woman was not small. She wasn't exactly *tall*, but she was taller than average, and she was broad. Her skin was darkened with the sort of tan of someone who spent most of their time out on the land, with sporadic patches of a slightly darker discolouration where she'd previously had frostbites. Was she a hunter? She could have been. She also had delicate but imperfect traditional tattoos etched on her face, done free-hand, very old fashioned. Perhaps on anyone else they'd be garish, but on this woman they were well-suited.

"I need a repair." The woman produced a beautiful, skillfully made sealskin pouch from her sleeve. She extracted some kind of jewellery from the pouch, but Akpa's sight blurred for a moment. Akpa rubbed her eyes once more, then tried to see what the woman brought. This time she could see that it was a pair of earrings.

The earrings were extraordinary. They were long, the length of Akpa's hand, and at first glance it seemed they were made with several different materials. Baleen and antler, with some feathers and seal claws dangling at the end.

Akpa grabbed a magnifying glass while the woman laid the earrings delicately down upon the white felt mat of the counter.

With the magnification, Akpa could see walrus whiskers dangling at the ends alongside the spotted white feathers and seal claws. There were many breaks throughout both earrings, and upon closer inspection she could make out that the small links connecting all the pieces together were made of a creamy white material. It took a moment for Akpa to figure out what the material was; it only clicked when she saw the actual earring hooks were also white.

"Tah! These are made of ivory?" There was no hiding the awe in her tone. These were the most exquisite pieces of jewellery she'd ever seen.

"Mmm," the woman murmured through a smug smile, her eyebrows raised in assent. "Yes. From the first narwhal I caught."

"Ivory from a narwhal tusk," Akpa mused. She looked over her glasses and stared at the woman, her jaw hanging wide open. There was no way she could compose herself. "How? Who made these?"

"I did," the woman said.

Akpa couldn't tell the woman's age. She wasn't young, but Akpa couldn't pinpoint how old she could possibly be. She didn't look like she was much older than her mother, but she also seemed ancient.

"Who are you?" Akpa asked.

Amusement spread over the woman's face as she answered, "My name is Kunuk."

Akpa's earlier feelings returned; terror mostly, mixed with curiosity.

"And you want me to repair these?" Akpa managed to say, surprised that she didn't stammer again.

"Yes," Kunuk said, entwining her fingers together. "You have made quite a name for yourself with your skill in mimicking exact replicas of the jewellery you've repaired in the past."

"I don't know if I'll be able to replicate these . . . " Akpa said, looking back, using tweezers to move the pieces around to get closer looks at them individually.

"Oh, you will," Kunuk said, leaving no room for negotiation.

"Well, I have no idea when I'll finish them," Akpa replied. "I already have several orders to fill. And I'll need a lot of room for error in trying to reproduce these pieces."

"You have until the end of the summer." A deadline, not a suggestion. "I do anticipate that you will have a hard time finding all the right pieces for this project."

"Summer? I'm sorry." Akpa shook her head. "I . . . I shouldn't take this on. I really don't think I'll be able to—"

"You will," Kunuk's tone shifted, hardened. She placed a cold hand on Akpa's shoulder. Akpa's eyes grew heavy then. She felt the hands guide her to the couch in the workshop and cover her in a blanket. "I will check your progress soon. Until then."

Akpa's eyes were closed when she felt a gust of cold air as the woman left the shack.

--\\\\<<<\\\\\\\\----

Akpa had no idea how long she'd feverishly slept, but the sky was brightening when she opened her eyes. Her father burst into the shed, a worried expression on his face. "Tah!" He lowered the temperature on the heater, looking around.

"What's your problem? Sleeping here! *Tukiqanngi*. Door wasn't even locked, stupid."

The heaviness in Akpa's eyes lingered, but she sat up. It was as hot as a sauna in the shed. "Sorry, I don't really remember how I—" She thought back. The gust of cold air, the feigned soft voice. Feelings of terror. She remembered a woman, larger than life. She puzzled through it all. "A customer came in last night . . . "

"You guys got wrecked or what?" her dad asked. "Atii! Get up, you gotta get in the house for a while. Close the shop for the morning, okay?"

Akpa agreed. She needed a shower and Advil. Her throat was dry and there was no amount of water on earth to quench her thirst. She stood and stretched, and from the corner of her eye, caught a glimpse of the earrings from last night.

Walking towards them, mesmerized, she remembered the woman's name was Kunuk.

There was no opportunity to linger. Akpa was practically thrown outside. With a last glance into the corner where the earrings sat waiting, she swore she felt something trying to pull her back. Her father slammed the door shut, locking it. Akpa felt the tension snap, her lungs filling with the air outside.

Once in the house, she made a post on her social media pages, "*Mamianaugaluaq*, the shop is closed today due to family emergency. I'll be back to the shop tomorrow. Qujannamiik."

Comments of support came throughout the day, but Akpa didn't bother to check or respond to them. She washed away the dust and grime that came with being in the shed all the time, nibbled on some frozen caribou and soya sauce, laid on the couch watching movies with her head in her mother's lap. Akpa took her parent's snowmobile and visited her best friend's house across town, where they sipped on some spiced rum and listened to loud music, dancing in her kitchen and playing cards. When her friend's kids started to get upset, Akpa drove back home bleary-eyed.

In bed, her thoughts kept going back to the earrings, remembering the tow she'd felt when she last glanced at them. Unable to avoid it any longer, Akpa snuck back out to the shed. She locked the door behind her.

- - - ⟨⟨⟨⟨⟨⟨⟩⟩⟩⟩⟩⟩ - -

Dozens of broken ivory chain links were strewn before her. Akpa didn't know how much time passed. When daylight leaked through the window, she didn't bother to unlock the door and she kept the curtains closed. If anyone stopped by, Akpa had no recollection. Her attention was focused solely on making the ivory links and hooks.

Drill, grind, snap. Over and over again, the ivory snapped. Drill, grind, snap.

It took days before she finally made enough pieces, and for her to finally hear the pounding at the door to realize she hadn't slept or eaten in as much time. Just as she was about to get up and open the door, it was knocked wide open, her brother stumbling into the shack with her mother and father behind him. They all stared at each other, her mother's face swimming with tears, the anger palpable on her father's reddened face.

Akpa hardly remembered the yelling that ensued. She was forced out of the shed, brought into the house, and given a bowl of soup.

"Look at you!" her mother bawled. "Your skin looks grey. How did you lose so much weight so fast?"

Akpa looked in a mirror to see a gaunt reflection, sunken cheeks, the bags under her eyes a deep purple. Almost unrecognizable.

Her father stood behind her mother, but his demeanor had changed from his earlier anger. Now he seemed shocked, his arms crossed, his mind seemed to be elsewhere. "Don't work on those." His voice was stern. "Give them back to the customer. Don't touch them."

Akpa glanced at her father. "What?"

"Don't touch them. Find her and return them."

"What's wrong?" Akpa's father was an easy-going guy, a jack of all trades who smoked weed most of his life. She'd never seen him like this.

"Those aren't what they seem. *Qanukiaq*. They're not right." He grabbed her arm. "Okay? Don't work on them again."

"I tried to say no. I tried to make her take them back." Akpa's voice sounded desperate, begging for understanding.

Akpa's mother, with her growing frustration, asked, "What are you even talking about?"

Her father shook his shoulders as if he had caught a sudden chill. "Ugh, the earrings she's working on. Something's not right. I got rid of them."

Something primal rose in Akpa's chest, trying to claw through. "Huh? What do you mean you got rid of them?"

Though there was little strength or energy within her a moment ago, Akpa stood inhumanly fast, and sped through the house to leave. In a matter of seconds, she was back in the shed, finding the ivory links and the rest of Kunuk's earrings mixed in the garbage can with coffee grounds and food wrappers.

The primal thing in her chest screamed. Akpa's throat had never made such a sound before, guttural and full of rage. She looked through the open door of the shed to see her family looking in, their eyes wide with terror. But their eyes were not focused on Akpa, instead they looked past her.

"Get to work," a soft voice spoke from behind her.

Akpa turned to see Kunuk there, wearing the same outfit, but the regal air about her had shifted into something more threatening. It hurt to look at her, so Akpa turned to the garbage can to retrieve the pieces her father had thrown out.

Kunuk walked toward the doorway, each step was heavy and shook the shed. Her voice, not smooth as silk anymore, was full of power. She demanded, "You will not disturb her work."

The door closed, and Akpa was alone.

She was able to salvage and clean most of the pieces she'd recovered from the garbage, but a lingering sense of wrongness filled Akpa for several days as she worked on the earrings. The dirtiness, though unseen, was stuck in her mind.

She scrubbed and scrubbed the pieces, breaking many of the ivory links she had tirelessly worked on. The baleen began to fray and peel, the antler began to disintegrate.

By the time she felt satisfied with the cleanliness, the pieces were unusable. She began to make the pieces anew, using baleen she'd gotten from the last community that had harvested a bowhead whale, antler pieces that customers had traded for payment, claws from the seals her father caught, whiskers from the walrus her grandfather had caught last summer. She'd gone out hunting for a day with her friend DJ to catch ptarmigans to use for the feathers.

In the meantime, her family brought her food to eat and helped to repair earrings for the other customers who had been waiting for their repairs for weeks. Soon, no one else was coming to get their earrings fixed. The gossip in town, shared in the aisles at the Northern store and Co-op, had shifted to the topic of Akpa's obsession.

Few people knew of Kunuk. Only Elders seemed to have any recollection of her, yet their memories of her were from their childhoods. Kunuk grew up with her grandparents at an outpost camp. They'd never moved into the settlement once it was established. Her family had evaded the RCMP's attempts to slaughter their dogs in an effort to force them into depending on the trading posts. Kunuk's grandfather had been known to have the abilities of an angakkuq.

As the settlement became more of a community, Kunuk and her grandparents were seen much less, for they were still nomadic and travelled with the seasons and the animals' migration. Akpa's grandfather remembered seeing Kunuk when he was out hunting as a teenager. She, too, was hunting, and she had three seals on her *qamutiik*. They had talked briefly, and he found that she was now living alone, her grandparents having passed away long ago.

"'Why not come to town?' I asked Kunuk. 'You don't have to live alone out here anymore.'" Akpa's grandfather told her. She was sat at her table, carving out the new ivory links and hooks. *Drill, grind, snap.*

"But Kunuk, she refused," Akpa's grandfather continued. "She said that being in town for too long would steal her life. She didn't need money. She ate the best food our land could offer, and she was a master of our traditional lifestyle. Real *inummarik*. She lived like the old ways. You know, I believe she inherited her grandfather's shamanic abilities. I believe she is one of the last *angakkuit* alive."

―――――――

It was only once she had made enough pieces of the ivory links again that Akpa realized she couldn't link them together. She swore, grabbed handfuls of her hair as the frustration flowed through her.

Her store of ivory was depleted.

She walked to DJ's house, unaware of the time or day. "Let's go hunting."

DJ, easygoing and unperturbed, said, "Tomorrow. I gotta get gas."

"Walrus hunting," was all Akpa said.

"Walrus?" DJ asked, taken aback. "It's not walrus hunting season."

"I need ivory."

"Doesn't change the season," DJ said.

"Okay, then we'll go to the floe edge. Catch a narwhal." She turned away to return home.

DJ called after her, "You're crazy!"

―――――――

DJ knew that he couldn't persuade Akpa—no one had been able to hold a meaningful conversation with her in months—so he found a group of more experienced hunters who were already planning to go to the floe edge. They tagged along the next day, hauling a small boat on a qamutiik.

They reached the floe edge, where seabirds floated on the calm water. The hunters had laughed almost into hysterics when Akpa mentioned that she wanted to catch a narwhal. She ignored them. They argued that it's not the season for narwhals, they were months and months away, but Akpa was convinced they would catch one.

It took hours and hours. The hunters had caught their fair share of game, seals for eating and for making new *kamiik* (sealskin boots). They were trying to convince Akpa that it was time to pack up when a puff of air spurted from the water.

The hunters, startled, became frantic. They scrambled to their machines and *qamutiit*. One of the hunters grabbed his rifle and took aim. He hit the whale with his first shot.

Everything happened with precision and skill. Though it was one of the hunters who had shot the whale, Akpa jumped into the boat and paddled out. She struck the whale with a harpoon and hauled it to the ice edge.

Once back to town, she took the tusk and went on her way. Back to the shed.

--·ıɪɪᶜᶜᶜᵗᵗᵗᵗᵗ·--

As she worked on the ivory links this time, Akpa used the utmost of care. She took no risk, pulling at every nerve of patience she possibly could. The task took months, with the finest of movements and tools. By the end, she had carved the ivory into chains, not just links. She meticulously carved tiny spiraling grooves into certain pieces so that they could be screwed.

She began attaching the pieces by screwing the ivory earring hook to the new disk of baleen, grinded down to five millimetres thick. She did the same with the rest, screwing the chains into the eight pieces of antler, reinforced with a fine piece of sinew collected from the tendons in the leg of a caribou. With tweezers and a magnifying glass, she tied a tiny knot, dipped a bit of seal fat, over the knot to strengthen it.

She attached the feather, whisker, and claw to the ends, like this as well, each knot dipped with seal fat.

She laid the earrings out in the sunlight for the fat on the knots to become sticky and harden.

Now that the last step to the earrings was done, Akpa felt as if she were lifting out of a daze. The sunlight seemed to pierce her eyes and she felt incredibly hot and sweaty, her clothing dingy. Looking through the window, she saw no snow on the ground. It was summertime. The purple fireweed and green moss covered the ground outside.

Akpa stumbled and fell.

How much time had passed? Akpa didn't know, but she woke to Kunuk kneeling next to her. Her cold hands were touching Akpa's shoulder. The sky outside, though still glowing with sunlight, had dimmed. It must have been late, but with the twenty-four hours of daylight in the summer, it was hard to tell what time it was.

"Qujannamiik, Akpa." Kunuk spoke softly, but not with kindness. Entitlement clung to the sound of her voice.

Akpa asked, "Are they good?"

"Ii, they will do." Kunuk confirmed. Kunuk took the earrings, putting them on. A glow seemed to come over her, as though the northern lights of the coming fall were shining down on her. She turned to leave, and at the door, Kunuk said to Akpa, "Rest now."

Akpa shut her eyes, and did not open them again.

VIII.

They began their farewells, but before Kipik disappeared, Jupi asked, "When will we see you next?"

Taken aback, the spirit's form burst for a second, and reformed into a fuzzier shape.

"Why do you ask?" Kipik retorted.

Maati's apprehension was palpable, she took hold of Jupi's arm, but he did not cower. In the depths of his being, Jupi knew that Kipik was an old friend, no matter how formal they acted in each other's presence.

"I only ask, old friend, because Maati is growing," Jupi said, his words measured. "Before we see you next, she might graduate high school. She might want to go to college. She might need to leave—"

Maati nudged her grandpa, interrupting him. "I'm not going anywhere."

Jupi looked at her, "What if you want to go to school, so you can get a good job? Maybe you don't want to get stuck up here like the rest of us?"

"I'm not stuck here," she said. "I love my home."

"Maati . . . " Jupi's voice was thick, speaking around a lump in his throat.

"You may risk what you would like to risk," Kipik spoke. "But it is too late for a new successor, Jupi, and you know the consequences if you come here without Maati next."

"What are the consequences?" Jupi asked. "Your memory is much better than mine. I do not remember."

Kipik bared their sharp teeth in a terrible smile. "Trust me that the consequences are excruciating."

Jupi made to speak again, but Maati nudged him to make him stop.

"*Tavvauvuti*, goodbye, Uncle Kipik," Maati said, "*Taku-kannilaarivugut*. We will see each other again."

"Smart one," Kipik said, then bid farewell.

Jupi and Maati did not speak as they did their clean-up routine, gathering their things, packing up, hiking back to where the boat was beached a few kilometers away. They waited for the tide to rise.

Maati was fuming, unable to speak through her anger.

Jupi, as much as he had grown with Maati, couldn't figure out the right thing to say.

The tide inched higher and higher, and they were almost ready to depart when finally, Maati asked, "Why did you do that?"

Jupi opened his mouth to speak, but the only sound that came out was an exasperated croak. He shrugged, tried again, "I—"

"Why would you do that?" she asked again. Her brow was furrowed, staring at the rising tide. Only a couple more minutes until they would jump into the boat and push off to head back to the cabin for the night.

"*Suuqaima*," Jupi said. "Because."

"Suuqaima?" Maati repeated. "What? You regret choosing me?"

"I just don't want you to get stuck here," Jupi echoed his thoughts from earlier, while Maati went to grab the boat's anchor a few meters away. "Me and your dad, we're stuck here. But you have so much ahead of you, you can become someone important, like your mom. You're very smart."

"But it's important for me to stay here," Maati said, putting the anchor on the bow of boat. "I've never felt like I fit in anywhere before. I've only ever felt like I belonged when I started coming here with you."

"But you don't have to," Jupi said. "If you want to go to school somewhere, you can go. If Kipik will punish me for letting you go, then I can live with it, but you don't deserve to feel like you have to stay here for this."

The tide was up. Maati jumped into the boat and found her spot in the passenger seat. Jupi pushed off the boat and jumped onto the bow. He took quick, measured steps and sidled into the driver's seat, starting up the motor and slowly maneuvering the boat through the shallow water before speeding off down the bay to their cabin.

When they slowed, reaching the shallow waters of their cabin, seeing Aatami sitting outside working on something or other, Jupi could see Maati trying to figure out what to say. It was obvious that she was still fuming.

He waited, slowing the boat almost to a halt.

"I just wish you would understand what I'm trying to say," Maati said. "I don't feel stuck here. I want to stay here forever. I love my home. I love my community. I love you."

"I love you, too," Jupi said.

Ukiaq | Fall

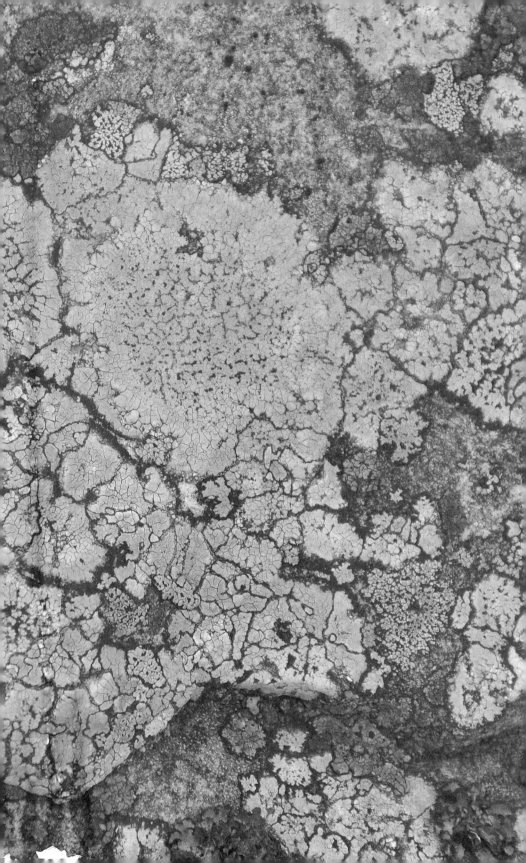

IX.

Over the years, Jupi's worries about Maati's future only grew. Though they tried to work things out, Maati avoided talking to him about her future at all costs. She suddenly remembered things she had to do, she visited him less and less. Sometimes the only time they would see each other was when they made their journey to the spot. They could both see how much Jupi had aged in so short a time span, but neither knew what to say.

Kipik, as always, visited sporadically. It was never predictable, the next time they would see the spirit.

When Maati graduated high school, Jupi went to her ceremony and couldn't hold back his tears. He'd never cried in front of another person since his wife's funeral, but his granddaughter walking across the makeshift stage in the high school gym with seven other graduates felt overwhelming. Afterward, when the grads were freed to take pictures with their families, Jupi and Maati hugged for a long time, the unspoken words over the years making the embrace feel heavy.

They went to the spot a week later, but Kipik did not appear.

A year passed.

Maati took courses online for a bachelor's degree in something—Jupi didn't really understand the English word and Maati couldn't really explain it in Inuktitut. It felt like a miracle when new Internet providers introduced unlimited Internet to the community, making her virtual classes manageable, no longer having to use up the however many gigs a month she and her mother had had to rely on before.

Jupi's age brought medical problems, and he'd go south for long bouts of time, for checkups and surgeries, but he remained relatively healthy otherwise. Sometimes, Maati would go on their long hunting trip alone, but still Kipik did not appear.

In the fall one year, the qulliq lighting fell on a day that Maati had an exam, and a day that Jupi was supposed to fly out to Ottawa after some worrisome blood tests. Both skipped these important events, ensuring that their duty to Kipik remained their priority.

It happened that Kipik appeared that day, seemingly knowing that both had risked skipping something that could affect their lives forever. The spirit, unsurprisingly, did not seem to care about the importance or inconvenience of what they had missed. The spirit asked only to hear another story.

Jupi spoke, "I am getting old. This journey is becoming too much for me. I would like to tell the story this time. I fear it will be my last."

Grumpy Old Man

Tumasi was fuming.

He'd gone to the community hall for Elder's Night. It was part of a string of themed events for the Christmas games season. There had already been Women's Night, Midnight Madness, and Men's Night. He'd gone to all the events he could go to. Every evening there was a different object being raffled off, a brand-new TV, an iPad or something, a new sewing machine. Tonight was a .223 rifle and bullets. He'd lost the other nights, but all he really cared to win was that rifle.

What made him angry, though, was a teenage girl who handed him a flyer at the door of the hall. She had a big silver piercing sticking out of the bottom of her lip, pink hair like bubble gum, and only half of her eyebrows! On top of that, she had three straight lines tattooed down the centre of her chin. He grimaced, then he looked down at the flyer, seeing only English words written all over the page.

"What am I supposed to do with this?" he asked in Inuktitut.

"Uhhh . . . " the girl said. "Sorry I—"

"*Tukisivinngaa*?" he asked. "Do you understand me?"

"Umm . . . "

He threw the piece of paper back at her. In the motion, as the page flipped over in the air, he could see the syllabic translations of the flyer on the other side. Unable to stop the momentum of his rant, however, he tacked on. "Take those stupid things out of your face. And wash that tattoo off. You can't even speak Inuktitut!"

He marched into the hall, looking for the table to enter his name into the raffle. His niece was at the table, handing out tickets with pens. He tried to scribble his name onto the tiny ticket, squiggly syllabics spelling out ᑐᒪᓯ. His niece deposited his ticket into the old Tim Horton's coffee urn with a slot cut into the top, wishing him luck. He saw the pink-haired girl move from greeting people to instead working in the canteen.

Tumasi roamed the hall, looking for a seat. Chairs lined the walls, but there were too many people scattered throughout the large room to all be seated. Luckily, Elders were prioritized in getting seats. The people that he knew were already seated and surrounded by friends and family who sat on the floor. They ignored him as he walked by.

The raffle was supposed to be at nine o'clock. Only a couple hours of this torture.

He found a spot in a darkened corner closer to the stage, next to people he vaguely knew but had no interest in conversing with. Some of them tried to make small talk.

"*Miali Kalasimasi*," someone said to him, wishing him an Inuktitized 'Merry Christmas.'

"Say, '*Quviasugit Quviasuvvingmit*,' instead," he replied. "You need to speak proper Inuktitut. Not this half-English nonsense."

The person nodded, then got up and moved somewhere else.

After a while, there seemed to be a bit of a radius around him.

The games began, but Tumasi never participated. Entering his name into the raffles was the extent of his participation at community events throughout the year. He could not believe some of the things the other Elders put themselves through during these events. Public humiliation and absolute debasement.

A group of Elders marched into the hall, wearing a myriad of trendy clothes: baggy pants, toques, crop tops, high heels, hoodies, chains, and beaded jewellery. They imitated the teenagers throughout the community, holding cellphones, some trying to twerk with rickety knees.

The crowd in the hall erupted into laughter, some people wiped tears from their eyes. Someone filmed on their phone, sharing live to social media the results as a group of judges tried to remain stone-faced, analyzing who the winner should be.

The winner was an old man with a blond wig under a knit hat with a red-yarned mohawk, wearing tight yoga pants that left nothing to the imagination, a pink crop top, holding a paper coffee cup in one hand, and a handbag in the other. On top of all that, he had traditional tattoos lining his chin and forehead.

Tumasi, somehow, grimaced harder. He did not approve of the young ones getting the traditional tattoos all willy-nilly, and he disapproved harder of the Elders who encouraged it. Despicable.

It was announced that the Elder won a barrel of gas.

In the next game, little grandchildren had to hold their grandparent in their lap, a reversal of roles, and feed them a bottle full of apple juice. The first duo to finish won a fancy vacuum.

It went on like this. Silly games where Elders were the laughingstock of the town. It was almost torturous, watching his peers get ridiculed and it being played off as a delightful game. Once, back in the old days, Elders were revered. Never questioned, their edicts followed, their wisdom sought. Now, they were nothing more than the butt of a ridiculous joke.

Tumasi's sister, Ooloosie, appeared in the seat next to him. She gave him a nudge, "*Aniapik*! My brother!"

He grunted, "Kaa."

"*Ajunngilatiit?*" she asked. "Are you well?"

He grumbled, not quite answering, then asked, "*Ivvilli?* What about you?"

"*Qanuinngittiaqtunga.* I'm wonderful."

Though they were less than a year apart in age, Ooloosie appeared years younger. Most of her hair was still black, only a few visible strands of salt. Sometimes, he resented her for this. She was always the one with no worries, always the one that others were drawn to. Tumasi was the one who always had to look after the family, always the hard-ass, the disciplinarian. No one liked him.

Granted, he didn't like anyone either.

Soon, a small group seemed to arrange themselves around Ooloosie. This always happened. Young folks flocked to her. She'd been an Inuktitut and Cultural Studies teacher at the elementary school for over thirty years now. The countless alumni of her classes always found her at community events, eager to tell her of the things they had done or achieved in the time since they last saw her.

"Ugh," Tumasi grumbled again. "Did you have to sit here? I can't see what's going on anymore."

Ooloosie laughed, slapping his arm playfully. "*Unaruluk.* You're not even enjoying the games anyway. Grumpy old man."

"Go sit somewhere else," Tumasi retorted. "I want to be able to hear the announcement of who wins the raffle."

"You'll be able to hear. Calm down." Ooloosie looked away, greeting more children as they passed her by. "Remember, Tumasi, games are supposed to be fun."

Eventually Ooloosie's husband joined them, and a few of her children, and several grandchildren. Ooloosie began to braid the hair of one of her many granddaughters.

Tumasi sighed, but he was ignored.

"Finally, we will announce the winner of the .223. Perfect for hunting seals and caribou, it comes with a soft carrying case and three boxes of bullets. Get your tickets out." There was a shuffling as people rifled through their pockets, retrieving their tickets. Ooloosie paid no mind, she continued braiding her granddaughter's hair.

"Okay, last three numbers, six, seven, four." There was a silence as people checked their ticket numbers. They called out the numbers again, in an Inuk accent, "Sixie-saipa-foa!"

Tumasi's last three digits were five, nine, five. He huffed his dissatisfaction, stood up to get ready to leave, but still the prize was unclaimed.

"Six-seven-four?" the numbers were called again. "Check your tickets! Sixie-saipa-foa!"

"Draw a new ticket!" Tumasi called.

"One more time, six-seven-four!"

An excited shout from beside Tumasi made him turn to look at Ooloosie as she held up a ticket.

"Sixie-saipa-foa!" She hopped up and down, weaved around the posse that was her family, and went on stage to claim the rifle.

Tumasi did not stick around, he was outside before Ooloosie even touched the prize.

----ᐊᒪᑕᑕ------

The next day, there was an Elders gathering at the visitor's centre. Tumasi sat off to the side, sipping tea, watching as others mingled.

The Real Elders, the ones who lived at the care facility and required day to day support, were wheeled into the centre. Tumasi watched as some of the women, including his sister, stood and offered to get the Real Elders tea. Gracious Ooloosie as always. Tumasi rolled his eyes so hard, he swore he almost sprained them.

One of the workers who had rolled the Real Elders in caught Tumasi's eye. He stared, her face covered in tattoos, a straight line down the centre of her chin, a deep V on her forehead, the point meeting between her brows, arrows pointing to her eyes on her temples, and a smattering of dots across her cheekbones.

The familiar anger boiled inside him, settling throughout his shoulders and chest. Before thinking, Tumasi was up on his feet, walking toward the woman.

"*Kinauvit?*" Tumasi asked. "Who are you?"

"Jocelyn," the woman replied, taken aback.

"Huh? Jasowan?"

"Jocel—"

He interrupted, "*Kinakkunnik angijuqqaaqaravit?* Who are your parents?"

"Miali *amma* Raapu Iqaluk. Mary and Robert Iqaluk," she answered.

Tumasi knew the Iqaluks. This woman's grandfather was one of Tumasi's childhood acquaintances. "Do they know about your tattoos? Your grandfather would be ashamed of you."

Even if he could have found a way to stop himself from scolding the girl, he wouldn't have. Tumasi was overwhelmed by the number of young women covering themselves in traditional Inuit tattoos without learning the meanings behind each symbol. He was sure that this woman didn't know what those tattoos meant, just as that pink-haired teenager from the Christmas games didn't know how to speak Inuktitut. He didn't understand why, and when he didn't understand something, it made him angry.

The tattoos were not needed anymore. When he was in his youth, they were told that the tattoos were demonic.

Well, they were also told that drum dancing and throat singing were demonic. In fact, they were told that most things related to their traditions were devilish and would send anyone to hell. But he could tell when some things were true and not, when some things were exaggerated, and he believed that tattoos were evil, though he knew that drum dancing and throat singing were not.

The woman did not say anything, but her pain was visible in her expression. An awkward silence followed.

The silence was broken, of course, by Ooloosie. "Tumasi, that's unkind."

Tumasi didn't say anything. His expression said enough.

Ooloosie went to the woman, laying a gentle hand on her arm, "Don't listen to him. He's just a grumpy old man. *Uvannulli tunnitit piujualuit.* To me, your tattoos are beautiful."

Tumasi shook his head. He grabbed his coat and left.

⋆⟨⟨⟨⟨⟨⟨⟩⟩⟩⟩⟨⟩⋆

It was a few days later when Ooloosie walked into Tumasi's house, announcing, "Merry Christmas!"

"Yup," he replied without looking up. He was intently listening to gospel songs on the radio. He was still mad at her for what had happened at the Elders gathering.

"Aren't you lonely?" Ooloosie asked.

He looked to her then, not knowing what to say. Lonely? Sure. Of course he was.

His wife was long passed away, his children gone to live in other communities. They rarely called him, even during the holidays.

He shrugged, "*Iiqai.* I guess so."

"Come to my house for supper tonight," she said. She

went over to him and hugged his side awkwardly as he refused to move from his seat, refused to embrace her back.

"Ugh," he replied. "I don't want to. I'm fine here."

She sighed. "Is this because of the other day?"

He brushed her off. "No. But how could you defend her? You know how I feel about it."

"Explain to me again why you don't want our young people to regain our culture," Ooloosie replied. "Our culture that was almost taken away from us!"

Tumasi's voice rose, "They are not regaining our culture, they are picking and choosing the parts that they like, forgetting the rest. Most young people don't even speak our language, what can you say about that? You are the one who should have taught them."

"It is not so simple, aniapik." Ooloosie shook her head in disappointment. "And being rude to our young people isn't going to teach them."

He did not reply; he was done with this conversation.

Ooloosie, however, was not. She cleared her throat, a false tone of positivity seeping into her voice. "I got you something."

She went into his porch, leaving the door open. "Shut the door!" he called after her.

She came back in, holding a long canvas case of camouflaged fabric.

"Tah," Tumasi said. Finally, he stood, walking over to get a good look at the rifle. The same one he had wanted to win so badly. He took it out of the case, "*Sulivii*? Really?"

She raised her eyebrows, nodding yes.

"Thank you," he said. For once, he couldn't find a reason to be angry.

"Please come to my house for supper tonight. My granddaughter is home for the holidays. We would like you to join us," she said. He nodded this time. "See you at church?"

He nodded again.

He didn't know what to do. It had been years since anyone had given Tumasi anything, and nothing as useful or great as a rifle.

Tumasi was not one to leave something unpaid or unacknowledged. But the stores were closed today. He went through his and his late wife's belongings, finding fox furs that were decades old—dried so badly from neglect that they were crumbling under his touch. He found sealskins in similar states, *uluit* covered in rust, stiffened fur clothing. Things he ignored and forgot about in the decades since his wife and children had left. Such a waste.

In a shoebox full of traditional tools in his shed, he found an old metal qulliq that he remembered was their grandmother's. One time, when he and Ooloosie were little kids, they had been alone at the outpost camp with their grandmother for a few weeks. Ooloosie would pick berries while Tumasi practised his bird calls and attempted to catch the birds with bolas.

The adults had made a trek to the settlement so that their mother could give birth to their new younger sibling.

One night, when it was pouring rain, the heat of the qulliq caused it to shatter in half. It had been an old lamp, passed down through generations.

Stranded without a lamp, Ooloosie and Tumasi, wet from the rain, whined about how cold it was. Their grandmother found an old tin can of beans scavenged from one of the old whaling ships close to their camp. She cut the lid off, poured out the beans to feed their dogs, and began hammering the lid.

She formed it into an oblong shape, flattening one end for a lip, indented the middle for the oil to gather. She lit the qulliq to warm up their *qarmaq*.

Tumasi had always loved his grandmother dearly, but that moment, he was inspired by her so deeply that he forever cherished whatever reminded him of her afterward. That fall, after their parents returned with his new sibling, bringing a proper qulliq back, Tumasi hid the qulliq with the few objects that were considered his. Some hunting tools he'd made with his father, harnesses he'd made for his future dog team. He used the qulliq when he was a young man learning to become a hunter. He saved it for years.

He fixed it up, polished the metal. He went to church, but his sister wasn't there.

That night, he brought the old qulliq to supper, wrapped in a plastic Northern bag. He walked into her house, full of many relatives that he hardly knew. All Ooloosie's family, and by extension, his.

The family didn't really engage with Tumasi. He didn't mind. He found his sister in the kitchen, stirring a pot of boiling seal meat.

He cleared his throat from behind her. "Ahem . . . Merry Christmas. Why didn't you go to church?"

Ooloosie turned around, a warm smile on her face.

Tumasi took a step back. Ooloosie had stark, black lines arranged in a double-V on her forehead. A slight redness bordered the black lines.

"Ugh!" Tumasi grimaced. "What have you done?"

Ooloosie grabbed Tumasi's hand. With her free hand, she gestured to the tattoo. "Aniapik, my brother, look! My oldest granddaughter gave me this today. That's why I didn't go to church."

He pulled his hand out of her grasp. "Shameful," he said. "Why would you do this to yourself?"

"Why wouldn't I?" she replied, unruffled by his response.

He walked away from her, leaving her house and family in a huff of his ever-present anger.

Twenty feet away, he heard her call his name, "Tumasi!"

He stopped, turning to look at her. She wore a green parka with black fox fur rimming the hood. Ooloosie, his lifelong companion, one of the few friends he'd ever had. She was the only person of meaning in his life that he saw regularly anymore.

And she betrayed him.

"How could you?" he said to her. "These tattoos. They are a thing of the past, they are evil. God does not approve of them."

"How could you say that?" she said. "God does not worry about such things. God loves everyone. He does not hate anything, He only forgives."

Tumasi shook his head and began walking away again. Ooloosie followed.

Again, he turned to look at her. In the cold air, frost covered the strands of Ooloosie's hair. She looked so much like their mother, but more so like their grandmother.

He remembered, then, that their grandmother had tattoos like the new one on Ooloosie's forehead. Not only that, but their grandmother had tattoos on her chin and cheeks, too, on her arms and legs.

Tumasi remembered now, wondering why he'd never noticed before how much Ooloosie looked like her.

"You look like *Anaanattiaq*," he said. Then, he remembered the plastic bag he was holding. He held it out to Ooloosie. "Here. Merry Christmas."

Ooloosie peered through the top of the bag, seeing the polished, old qulliq. "Anaanattiaq's qulliq? You kept it all this time?"

"Hmpf."

"My grumpy brother," Ooloosie said, embracing him properly. For the first time in years, he hugged back. "You need to let go."

He looked at her face again, at the stark new lines on her forehead. He didn't know what he felt, but he enjoyed being reminded of their grandmother. Perhaps he might someday be used to the tattoos. Perhaps they would become as common as they had been when he was little. Finally, he replied, "*Aksut*. I agree."

The two siblings, who had known each other their whole lives, who had lived in the same town their whole lives, who were opposites of each other, but still friends, walked arm in arm, back to the warmth of Ooloosie's house.

X.

They sat, as they often did, in silence. Letting the end of the story take hold, the three of them made no move to conclude the visit. The cold autumn air was masked by the bright midday sun. It had already begun its descent to the horizon.

There was a long pause, none of them making a gesture to move.

The lingering quiet was full of emotion. They all knew that this was a goodbye. Even telling the story seemed to have aged Jupi further. His mouth was dry from all the speaking. He coughed to clear his throat, but it didn't seem to dislodge whatever discomfort he was feeling. Even his breath came out beleaguered.

Finally, Maati moved and grabbed a Thermos from her bag. She handed the lid to Jupi to use as a cup. She unscrewed the top, the vapour and aroma of hot coffee wafted out. She poured the coffee into the cup. Gratefully, Jupi took a tentative sip.

Jupi downed the coffee, then made to stand. Maati took hold of Jupi's arm to help him up.

Kipik remained sitting, staring at Jupi.

"You've been a good companion, old friend." Kipik spoke in a gentle tone, softer than Jupi had ever heard them speak.

"Ii," Jupi said. "You too. You have taught me so much, though it took me too long to learn your lessons."

"It took just the right amount of time," Kipik said. "And you are leaving your task in good hands. Your granddaughter is who we have waited for, for all this time."

"Ii," Jupi agreed. For the first time in their whole friendship, Jupi turned his back on Kipik, beginning his trek home. He turned for one last look. "Tavvauvuti, Kipik. Goodbye."

"Tavvauvuti," Kipik said, vanishing in the light once again.

Jupi kept walking as Maati cleaned and packed up. It only took her a moment to catch up to him, though he did get farther than she thought he would. There was still some of that liveliness left that Jupi was known for. A fit old man, but it was still a long hike.

The wind picked up, making the swells too big for them to boat back to their cabin.

Maati had been prepared for this. While Jupi sat on a rock, she set up a small tent, a pop-up style that was usually used for ice fishing. She secured it down, hammering pegs into the soft, mossy tundra, then she laid out some sleeping bags and a Coleman stove.

During high tide, Maati and Jupi watched over the boat, careful that it didn't smash into the rocks of the shoreline, or drift too high up onto the beach. Once the tide lowered, they retreated into the tent, boiling some water to eat some cups of instant noodles.

There wasn't much to say. Jupi told Maati about his life, about his meetings with Kipik over the years.

"It was hard to think of all those stories for so long. Since I was ten! How old am I now?" Jupi thought deeply.

"One hundred?" Maati teased.

"Ah!" he pushed her. "No way."

"Oh!" Maati said. "Did I say hundred? I meant thirty-three."

"Yeah, that's more like it," Jupi agreed. They laughed with no worries, for the first time since that summer when she was fifteen. Since then, their interactions had been tense. It had become a huge strain just to have a conversation that didn't turn into pain.

Maati regretted the last five years of avoidance. She should have forgiven her grandfather; he was only wishing for her a future unburdened.

"Ittuq," Maati said, "tell me a story."

"I can't tell stories no more," Jupi said. "I'm all used up."

"I don't believe that." She nudged him.

"You know, one time, I started telling Kipik a story

about Sanna, or like the qallunaat call her, 'Sedna,' but Kipik stopped me, saying that I already told that story. I said, 'Not even! I told you about Nuliajuk!'"

Maati furrowed her brow, "But . . . aren't they the same story?"

"That's what Kipik said," and Jupi burst into laughter.

The wind died down overnight, and they went back to town, passing their cabin—Aatami no longer had to accompany them on their trips. Back in town, they towed the boat back to Jupi's house and unpacked their supplies.

Maati moved out of her mom's house, moving into Jupi's. She fixed it up the best she could. She harassed the housing corporation until they made proper repairs on the windows, walls, and floors, then she ordered new couches and other furniture, got new plates and bowls and cups.

Jupi went back and forth to Ottawa for cancer treatment. He no longer worried about going to meet Kipik. Maati was able to do that task on her own, but the spirit did not come back for quite some time.

Jupi passed away two years later. Maati was holding his hand.

"I waited for you all my life," Jupi had told her moments before his last breath, grasping her hand firmer than he had for a long time. "You were always the one I was waiting for."

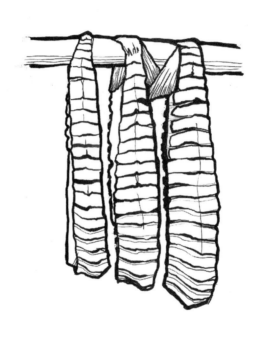

Uking | Winter

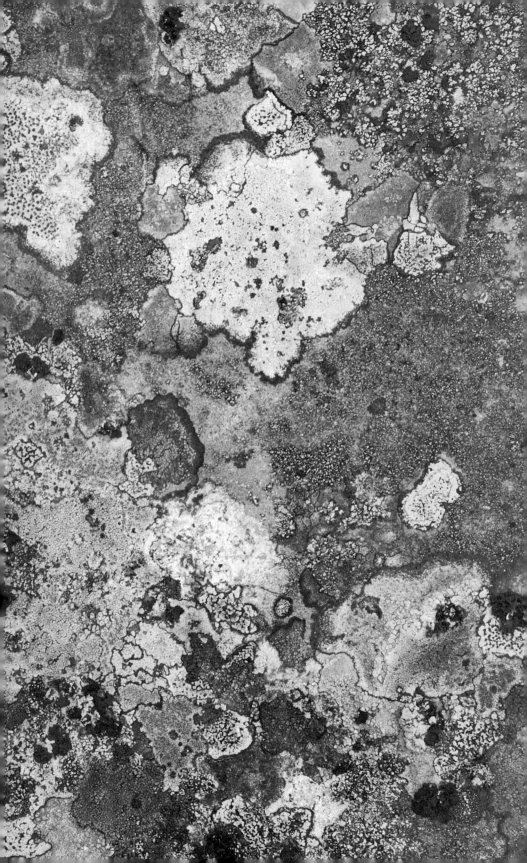

XI.

Maati managed to carry on. After Jupi died, she moved back in with her mom, while her father and Uncle Mark found places to stay until their names were higher up on the housing wait-list and new units became available.

Season after season, she did her calculations, planned her trip to the spot, hiked there alone, lit the qulliq.

Kipik did not reappear for years.

She finished her studies, got her bachelor's degree in sociology. She got a job with the Government of Nunavut that came with housing. She got a boyfriend, an old high school classmate who had gone off to college and come back home with big dreams to make change in their community.

Maati never told anyone about Kipik. Her mother often questioned why Maati still made the trip every season, no matter what the forecast was, even in the dead of winter when it was mostly pitch-black outside for twenty-two hours a day. She merely said that she did it to feel closer to Jupi.

If anything, Jupi's death made her closer than ever with her father. Aatami often stayed with her for long stints when he was tired of couch surfing. When Maati's boyfriend was out of town for a conference one time, Aatami and Maati had stayed up late to watch a *Lord of the Rings* movie marathon.

"Did you know he broke his toe when he kicked that helmet? That's why his scream is so good, he was actually in pain," she informed Aatami.

Her dad only laughed, watching the movies mostly to appease her. "Oh yeah?"

She'd fallen asleep not too long after that. When the credits were rolling, Aatami nudged her awake.

"Can I tell you something?" he asked.

Groggy, she nodded.

"When I was ten, my dad brought me to meet Kipik," Aatami said.

Her heartbeat quickened, eyes widening. "What?"

"He took me," Aatami continued. "Friggin' hard work to get there. My oldest brother, Jacob, used to go there with him, but he ended up killing himself when he was sixteen."

Maati had only heard of her Uncle Jacob a handful of times, but she didn't know anything in depth about him other than how he died.

Her father kept going. "My dad tried to bring Mark, but he had to leave him at the cabin. Mark was always too crazy. He got into drugs really bad after Jacob died. When I turned ten, my dad brought me, but I think I cried too much. He never took me again."

"You went there with him?" Maati asked. "I always thought Ittuq never brought anyone."

"I think he forgot," Aatami said. "I think he wanted to protect us."

"How come you never told me?" Maati asked.

"I didn't want to think about it," he said. "I've never been so scared of something in my life. I think that's why he never brought it up, too. The way I shut down about it, I think he started pretending that it never happened, then I think he really believed that it never happened."

Maati didn't know what to say.

"My dad, he was a really good dad, and I really trusted him with you," Aatami said, tears welling in his eyes. "I feel bad that me and my brothers weren't good sons. He's lucky you came along. I keep thinking about that."

"He loved you guys," Maati said, crying too. "I think he didn't want to burden anyone, even me."

"*Inummarialuulaurmat,*" Aatami said, wiping tears and snot away. "He was a real Inuk, you know? A good person. Traditional, strong, but able to change. He was adaptable, and he really cared about the good of the family. Just like you. Me and my brothers aren't like that. We got stuck in our ways very early in life. That's why we couldn't carry on the tradition of going on the long hunting trip."

Maati was lost for words, struggling to find something

to say, but her father was carrying on, unleashing years of bottled-up feelings and emotions.

"You know, if you're literal in your translation of 'inuk' it means 'to be alive.' But in our culture, to be Inuk is to always try to be a good person. Not just to be alive, but to help others live. That's what my dad was. That's what you are. It's no wonder you're the one that can face Kipik. You're very brave."

"That's what Ittuq Jupi told me, the first time he took me there," Maati remembered. "He told me I was brave."

"Suuqaima," Aatami said. "Because."

Time passed. Maati and her boyfriend got married at the small Anglican Church. They had a little boy.

She was beginning to wonder if the spirit would ever return. When finally Kipik reappeared, Maati's hair was just starting to grey.

Kipik greeted her, "Maati."

"Kipik," Maati replied. From behind her, a small boy's face peeked around. Maati smiled. "This is my son, Jupi."

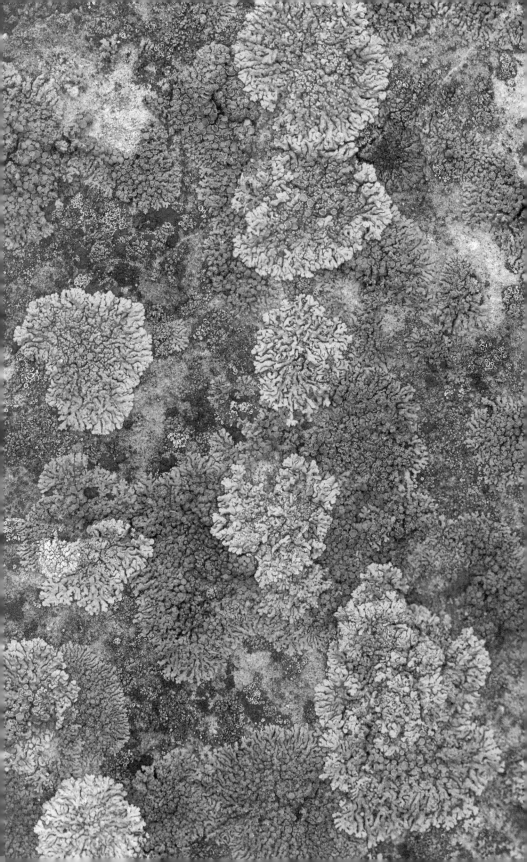

Mussels and Qunguliq

Author's note: Nunavik and Qikiqtani dialects of Inuktut are quite different. In this story, the dialects are referred to with their regional spelling of the language, i.e., Nunavik speaks Inuttitut, whereas Qikiqtani (North Baffin, Nunavut) speaks Inuktitut.

An old woman lived in a shack at the top of the town on a cliffside. In the summers, when Taisy would go to visit her grandfather in Nunavik, she would find herself drawn to the old lady. She would often walk from her grandfather's house along the sloping road uphill to the airport before taking the left turn around the arena, then up past the radio station, to go see her.

"What's that old lady's name, *Ataatatsiak*?" Taisy had asked her grandfather in broken Inuttitut, pointing toward the top of the cliff.

"Angusaaruk," was his answer.

Taisy couldn't really speak or understand Inuttitut, especially since the dialect they spoke in Maktaaq City was different. She confused the meanings and the pronunciations, finding herself thinking too hard and missing the conversation entirely. This didn't diminish any love between herself and her grandfather, though. She could communicate with him just fine without speaking. His goofy and affectionate nature translated across their differing languages. He flipped his dentures in his mouth as a gag that resulted in her giggling until her belly hurt. He paid her a dime for every white hair she plucked from his scalp.

The lady—Angusaaruk—was stoic and had little humour etched into her. Even the wrinkles on her perpetually pursed upper lip seemed to be carved from immovable stone. Their communication was limited in almost every sense, but there was a deep fondness between the two.

Taisy was named after the old lady, her middle name tying them together.

Angusaaruk tended to the area surrounding her shack with the utmost care. She called the little girl *"sauniq"* to signify their common name, their shared spirit. Taisy would often find her bent over at the hips, gently placing new stones on the ground or plucking a stray plant from between the rocks. In front of and around the shack, the ground was lain with thin, flat rocks, found peeled from larger shale boulders, and meticulously placed to make a beautiful mosaic. In the centre of it all, there was a decades-old hearth of soot-covered rocks, an iron rack splayed across, with an old, blackened kettle sitting atop. *Innirviit*, wooden frames for stretching animal hides, leaned against the shack, secured in place with rope to save them from falling over during windy days.

Angusaaruk always had a hand-rolled cigarette hanging from her lips, and though Taisy didn't like the smell, she sometimes felt comforted by it. The old lady wasn't tall, but she was a big woman with a big bum. She wore a purple Ukrainian granny scarf, wrapped around her head like a bonnet, and hefty rubber boots, rain or shine.

Taisy liked to bring Angusaaruk mussels she scoured from the seaweed, or *airaq*, the roots of plants that she liked because they tasted like dirt, or *qunguliq*, a juicy red plant with sour leaves. In exchange, Angusaaruk gave her bannock and always had a stash of junk food at the shack.

The old woman had many people coming and going for trades, for she dealt in many things that could not commonly be found, such as *naluaq*, sealskin leather that was freeze-dried white in the winter, or *iqaqti*, black sealskin leather, or *atungatsaq*, the thick skin of bearded seals used for the soles of sealskin boots, *kamiit*. She was able to make a living selling skins she worked on and kamiit she made. She taught others how to make them, too.

Over the years, the shack became a refuge for Taisy. She did not have many friends in this town. She only visited in the summers, and she found it hard to try to make the same kind of friendships that her siblings did. Her cousins were rambunctious and sometimes mean, and Taisy did not want to spend all her time clinging to her mother. Ataatatsiak would often take her brother, uncles, and cousins out hunting or to the cabin, while her sister would spend time with friends and boyfriends.

As Angusaaruk aged, Taisy began to help her tend to the rocks and plants around the shack, helped to hoist and secure the sealskin stretchers to the little house. She would help make the bannock and watch over the boiling meat on the hearth. Sometimes, she even brought some of Angusaaruk's clothing home to be washed.

It was rare that Taisy ever came to her mother's hometown in the winter, but the year she turned twelve, they came for Christmas. By then, Taisy was better at making friends, and even found herself comfortable in crowds. She wasn't embarrassed to follow her siblings around anymore, and she took it in stride when they made jokes at her expense rather than taking the jokes to heart.

The day they arrived, she followed her siblings to the school gym where Christmas games and dances were held, and she looked for the old lady amongst the crowd. It appeared, though, that Angusaaruk was not present, even though it seemed that the whole community had gathered for the holiday festivities.

That year at school, Taisy had a new Inuktitut teacher and she'd learned a lot in the past semester. Not only was she speaking more and more of her mother tongue, but a firmer sense of security and belonging came with it. Taisy was excited to see Angusaaruk and to communicate with more than a plethora of gestures and a few words of mutual understanding sprinkled in.

Taisy bundled up warmly the next day, putting on snow pants that belonged to her aunt, who was two years younger than her, and a pair of boots belonging to one of her cousins, her parka, hat, mitts, and a scarf. As she stepped out of her grandfather's house, her teenage uncle was sat on the snowmobile, smoking.

"Where you going?" he asked. Uncle Josiah was wearing nothing more than a windbreaker, sweatpants, and running shoes.

"Angusaaruk's," was all Taisy said. Uncle Josiah was a terror to her older siblings, but Taisy was privileged because she was younger. Surely it had nothing to do with her tendency toward tattling.

The walk up the hill was rigorous in the winter. The roads icy, sometimes piled with large snowdrifts. The road was much less travelled, she could see. Hardly any trails, all of them days old and not maintained.

She arrived at the top of the hill in a huff and felt the sweat in her armpits and her back soaking into her layers of clothing. The sight of smoke wafting from the chimney of the familiar shack brought an overwhelming sense of relief to Taisy. Suddenly emotional at the sight, she rushed toward the house, impatient to see her old lady friend for the first time in winter.

Her knock on the door was answered with a note of confusion. Knocking was not a common practice here, and it usually meant that a qallunaaq was on the other side of the door. Taisy made her way inside, finding Angusaaruk sitting in her bed with an old-fashioned Game Boy Color in her hands. It was purple. The Elder put the game down, her eyes narrowed as she tried to place who had come to visit.

"*Angusaaruungai,*" Taisy greeted, feeling a little out of place. "Hi, Angusaaruk."

"Aa," Angusaaruk answered in hesitation. Still, she squinted, not recognizing the young girl.

"It's me," Taisy went on, pronouncing her name the way the old lady did, "Tiisi."

"Tiisi?" Angusaaruk echoed. Her eyes lit up with recognition. "Aa! *Sauniapiingai! Sugami tamaaniikkit?* Hello, my beloved namesake! What are you doing here?"

Relief flooded through Taisy. Unknowingly, she had been afraid that she'd be forgotten. Last summer, Angusaaruk had started experiencing lapses in memory. She'd sometimes call Taisy by the names of her own children, Arnaara, Jusipi, or Pavvik. Taisy smiled wide, proudly speaking Inuttitut, "*Quviasuvviksiuriaqtunga*. I came here for Christmas."

Taisy's Inuttitut speaking went unnoticed. Angusaaruk asked her to fill a cup with water, then asked if she could help to tidy up the little shack.

The inside of the shack was humble and cozy. A bed was tucked into one side and there was a counter on the other side. Various tools were hung on the walls, uluit, an axe, handheld scrapers and stretchers for sealskins, interspersed with printed photographs and clippings from newspapers, airplane magazines, and other publications. A fire was blazing in the wood stove, a stack of shipping pallets cut up into kindling off to the side. Taisy grabbed a mug and filled it from a bucket of fresh water. She handed it to the old lady.

After months of practicing Inuktitut, Taisy finally tried to initiate a conversation. She started with a question she had always wanted to ask: "*Sugami tappaannialuk illuqaqpit?* Why is your house way at the top of the cliff?"

Angusaaruk smiled, a rare sight that made Taisy feel warm inside. She answered, "*Aatsuuk, taimaippuq*," which, to Taisy's interpretation, meant, "I don't know, that's just the way it is."

This was a common way for Elders to reply. Taisy was realizing this as her language skills improved and she pushed herself to talk to Elders more. She was often answered with, "That's the way it is."

For a while, the two sat together in an awkward but not uncomfortable silence. Eventually, Angusaaruk patted a spot next to her on the bed. Taisy obliged, taking a seat so close to the Elder that she could smell the musk of cabin life from her, and looked at her expectantly. The old lady leaned over the side of the bed, opening a cookie tin filled with knick-knacks, and produced a necklace that could have been a relic, the centrepiece an ivory amulet carved in the shape of an *inuujaq*, an old-fashioned doll that Inuit used to make out of driftwood. She put it over Taisy's head, the necklace resting on her chest.

Angusaaruk spoke, but Taisy couldn't catch all that she said, her Inuttitut skills not quite up to speed. "This will help you," was the gist of Taisy's understanding.

She thanked the Elder, peering at the amulet more closely, running her fingers over the smooth ivory. Taisy looked at Angusaaruk, "Wow!" she said. "*Piujuq*! It's beautiful!"

The Elder smiled, then patted Taisy's head. There was a clear affection in the old lady's eyes, a look that Taisy hadn't seen from her before. Though the two had grown close and fond of each other over the years, Angusaaruk rarely showed any emotion.

Taisy rose and got ready to leave. Angusaaruk handed her a bag of bannock before she left.

The next day, Taisy returned to find the door to the shack swung wide open, a snowdrift forming in the doorway. She peeked inside, only to see a heap on the bed. Taisy screamed and rushed back home, finding her grandfather at the kitchen table.

"Ataatatsiak! *Angusaarukkunnit* . . . Angusaaruk . . . " she was crying, unable to form words, a sentence. She didn't know what she had seen, she didn't know how to communicate that.

Her mother, bleary-eyed from a late-night card game with her childhood friends, rose from the couch. "It's too early for this, *piipii*. What are you trying to say?"

"Angusaaruk's house!" Taisy tried to gather her thoughts. "The door was open. I think something happened."

Her mother stood, clear concern over her face. She told Ataatatsiak in Inuttitut what Taisy had said and told him to go and check on the old lady. Ataatatsiak left in a hurry and drove up on his Ski-Doo. Taisy's mother called the police, while Taisy, unsure of what was happening and what she was feeling, cried and cried into her mother's chest.

It was a somber Christmas. Taisy and her family returned home before Angusaaruk's funeral was arranged.

Her trips to visit her grandfather were never the same. She would find herself staring out the kitchen windows, toward the slope that led to Angusaaruk's old cabin.

Her cousins still bullied her, her siblings still found their own things to do. Nothing had changed except that Angusaaruk was gone, making it so that everything had changed. Taisy had no desire to scour the seaweed and shoreline for mussels, she no longer dug for roots. The only thing she still did was pick qunguliq, the sourness of the leaves still satisfying her.

Taisy clung to the necklace that the old woman had given her, only taking it off when she was going to bathe. She changed the cord multiple times—it broke often—before finally saving up enough money from her chores to buy a good chain. If she took it off for longer than a couple hours, anxiety would slither through her. For years, Taisy hid the necklace under her shirts, not wanting attention drawn to it, clinging to the memory of Angusaaruk.

She had been told that nothing bad had happened to the old lady, only that she passed away peacefully in her sleep. Taisy felt some comfort by this, but not much.

It all just felt like too much and too late. Taisy had only just started speaking Inuttitut, she had only just started gaining confidence. Those feelings shattered, the urge to learn vanishing with Angusaaruk. They had only distant blood relation, yet there had always been an underlying spirit linking them, the name they shared.

Taisy had been named after the old lady, but she had never gone by that name. In fact, Taisy was named after several people. She had a handful of middle names she did not often use. She had established herself quite firmly only as Taisy. Elders and her mother's friends had called her by endearment terms all her life, like "little mum" or "little brother" or "my wife," but she did not truly associate herself with those names.

When she started college, Taisy introduced herself to her professors and classmates as Angusaaruk. When they sputtered at the name, butchering the word, Taisy did not retreat to her easier-to-pronounce first name. She made them address her properly. She did not let them slide with nicknames, and she always corrected their mispronunciations or misspellings.

With the distance from home grew her desire to retain everything about her culture that she could. In the margins of her textbooks, Taisy wrote notes in syllabics, sometimes nonsensical, just trying to hold on to it. She called and texted her mom in a mix of several Inuktut dialects, which her mother often corrected. When she didn't know how to say a certain thing in her language, she roamed the internet for Inuktut glossaries.

As time went on, the open wound of losing Angusaaruk began to fade. She became friends with her cousins, rather than thinking of them as bullies. They laughed about their time together as kids, the sensitivities of childhood no longer overwhelming, nostalgia taking over instead. They often found themselves poking fun at each other.

Once, when Taisy was back home for the summer, she'd taken the necklace off for longer than she ever had before, leaving it on her dresser. She'd gone to visit friends without it, and when she got back home, the necklace was gone.

She tore her room apart, checked every nook and cranny of the house. When she found her sister wearing the necklace, Taisy's brain almost broke. She took it from her sister's neck, to which her sister only laughed.

"My saunik gave this to me," Taisy said. "Don't ever touch it again."

"Geez," her sister said. "It's not that deep."

The dismissal made Taisy want to cry, the sleeping pain awoken. She didn't cry, though. She had closed that part of herself off long ago, and she did not want to reopen it.

"Can I borrow your necklace?" her sister asked not too long after. "For my trip to Toronto? I feel like it would really go with the look I have planned for the concert."

Taisy had never felt herself grimace so hard. "No."

Her sister was not deterred, begging for weeks, but Taisy also never wavered. "I've kept the necklace secret for so long for a reason."

But sisters are often closer to each other than any other relationship. As time went by, the more they became the same person. Perhaps Taisy did not lend her the necklace that time, but she did another time.

The regret of lending was almost immediate, an underlying discomfort overtaking her in an instant. Before her sister's flight even landed, Taisy was wishing for the necklace back.

She thought back to when Angusaaruk gave her the necklace, and in Taisy's unfamiliarity with the language, she had missed most of what Angusaaruk had told her. All she remembered was that Angusaaruk had said, "This will help you."

Thinking hard, Taisy tried to remember what the old woman had told her. She thought, perhaps, that their shared spirit had joined her, and she remembered more clearly, with her deeper understanding of the language, what the Elder had told her.

"I made this for you. I was going to tell my daughter to give it to you, but you're here now." She remembered Angusaaruk's hands, calloused from the hard work of skinning seals and frying bannock, pushing the necklace into her hands. "I'm getting old, and I hope this will protect you."

It had been thirteen years. A long, long time.

Maybe the necklace hadn't protected her, but it had brought her a sense of security. It had brought her connection.

When Taisy's sister brought it back, Taisy swore to herself she would never part with it like that again. She framed the necklace, brought it dorm to dorm, apartment to apartment, house to house.

When finally she gave it to one of her distant namesakes, she told them, "My saunik, Angusaaruk, gave this to me.

"She has been gone for so long, but I thought of her every day. I still think of her. She was beautiful. She did not tell me with words that she loved me, but I knew it every day that she did.

"When you wear this necklace, when you look at it, know that I love you, and the Angusaaruk that we are named after loves you, too. She has grown to know you through me, and I hope that we will know and love your namesakes through you."

XII.

Maati, surprisingly, was stoic as she came to the end of her story. Her little son was off to the side, fiddling with makeshift toys from the land. Rocks, mostly.

Kipik did not speak for a long time, and Maati did not either. Their silent revelry was only interrupted by the child's playing, but not distractingly so. Maati's little Jupi was much like her, finding ways to entertain himself without bothering the adults.

"I've observed you for most of your life," Kipik said. "I am not surprised that you continued to come here after my old friend left, but I am comforted by it."

"It is the task I was given," she said. It was a matter of fact.

Her life, for over twenty years now, had been consumed with the duty to light the qulliq. To learn as much as she could about living off the land, about learning the environment they lived in, about her ancestors, about relearning her language and revitalizing traditions and customs that were almost lost to colonization. It was just how she lived now, not second nature, but the basis of her every movement.

"Did your grandfather ever tell you why this task was bestowed on your family?" Kipik asked.

Maati shook her head, scrunching up her nose. "I don't know if he knew, or I think he had forgotten by the time I came around."

Kipik smiled, genuinely. Maati was not frightened by the spirit's vertical features, and she had warned her young son of the spirit's eerie nature. The boy paid the two of them no mind, focusing only on the rocks and lemming skeletons that he had dug up.

"I was once a caribou," Kipik said.

Maati knew, now, that it was finally Kipik's turn to tell their story.

"I allowed myself to be caught by your ancestor. He had been so hungry, but his family was hungrier, starving at their camp, close to where your grandfather's cabin is.

"Your ancestor, I could tell, would not eat my flesh until his family ate, so I allowed him to catch me. I only asked that he leave my skull and antlers undisturbed, right here on this beach.

"But your ancestor, he came back for me. He wanted my antlers so that he could make tools for his sons. In other cases, I would have cursed your ancestor, haunted him until he died. I did not feel that was appropriate."

"You still cursed him though," Maati said, coming to an understanding. "Not haunted, but still."

"I gave him a duty," Kipik agreed. "To continue to meet me, to tell me stories. But still, I did not feel appeased."

She took it in, imagining the beach once an easy area for hunting. She imagined a man who looked much like her Ittuq Jupi, but without his thick, tinted glasses. She pictured him telling traditional stories, myths and legends to her now, but back then they had been the equivalent of scripture. For years, she had been telling these stories, but for millennia it had been her many grandfathers telling their own.

"Am I the first woman?" she asked.

"Yes, but that is not why I am telling you this now," Kipik said. "It is more because men tend to only trust their burdens onto other men."

Maati waited, no questions. She knew, deeply, that Kipik would not leave her with any lingering inquiries. They would answer all that she needed to know.

"Your grandfather, at one time, was told that he needed to continue the duty to see me because the world would end if he didn't," Kipik continued. "That is what the task came to mean to your family.

"But after three failed attempts with his sons, my dear old friend Jupi almost became resigned for the tradition to end with him.

"He'd forgotten, I knew, the importance of the tradition.

It was evident in his sons. I am aware that life is very different for you humans now. But life here is important, my dear. It may change, but it cannot be forgotten, what your ancestors went through. That is why I tasked your kin with this."

"You did not want it to be forgotten. Our practices, our skills," Maati replied.

"Yes. But more so than that, I did not want it forgotten how strong your people are. And when you arrived, I knew we were in good hands," Kipik said. "When I said goodbye to Jupi, it was also meant as a goodbye to you."

"Was it?" Maati squinted her eyes.

"Well," Kipik smiled, "it could have been."

Maati looked at her son. He was used to adults, used to them having big conversations where he didn't understand half of what was said. He needed a sibling, she realized.

"But you continued the duty," Kipik went on. "You were taught well."

"Perhaps if I stopped coming, the world would have ended," Maati answered the unasked question. "I was never told this, but that is what I assumed. Even then, I think it is how I realized the importance of being Inuk."

"And what is that?" Kipik asked.

"The importance of being Inuk?" Maati asked, but she continued with her own answer. "It is, as it always has been, to be a good person, and to help others live."

Kipik's smile, which had always been difficult to inter-pret, was now gladly open. "And your grandfather taught you that?"

"No," Maati said. "Actually, my father did."

"Jupi was a good man," Kipik replied. "I told him that it was you that we were waiting for, but it was actually him."

Maati could not hold it back anymore, tears welling in her eyes. Her grandfather's last words to her had been that he had been waiting for her.

"It was not that he was waiting for me," she realized aloud. "It was that he only realized who he was, and what his role was, when I came along."

"Yes," Kipik agreed. "I could have left you coming here, cursed your bloodline to keep coming here for centuries more."

"But my Ittuq Jupi was your friend," Maati smiled through her tears.

"Yes," Kipik said. "So I will now say goodbye. For good. Do not forget what you have learned here."

"Mm," Maati sniffed, "I'll make sure my son can tell the story of Sanna. Like his namesake."

Kipik's smile faltered. "Make sure he learns more than that one story, too."

Maati laughed. "I know."

Kipik vanished in a trick of the light, as always, and Maati cleaned up. She moved to grab the ancient qulliq, how many generations had it served? It crumbled to dust at her touch.

Glossary of Inuktut Words

The pronunciation guides in this book are intended to support non-Inuktut speakers in their reading of Inuktut words. These pronunciations are not exact representations of how the words are pronounced by Inuktut speakers. For more resources on how to pronounce Inuktut words, visit inhabitmedia.com/inuitnipingit.

Inuktitut Term	Pronunciation	Meaning
aaka	ah-KAH	no
aakkai	ah-KAH-ee	no way
aamai	ah-MAH-ee	I don't know, or I'm not sure.
Aatsuuk, taimaippuq	aaht-SOOK TAH-ee-mah-eep-pook	I don't know, that's just the way it is.
aiin	AH-een	endearment
airaq	AH-ee-rahk	the roots of a plant
Ajunngilatiit?	ah-YOON-gee-lah-teet	Are you well?
aksut	ahk-SOO	I agree
amauti	ah-MAH-ootee	woman's parka with a pouch for carrying a child
amma	ah-MAH	and
anaanattiak	ah-NAH-naht-tee-ahk	grandmother (Inuttitut dialect spelling)
angakkuit	ah-ngahk-KOO-eet	shamans
angakkuq	ah-ngahk-KOOK	shaman

Angakkuuvungaqai?	ah-ngahk-KOOP-oon-gahk-ah-ee	Maybe I'm a shaman?
angusaarukkunnit	ah-ngoo-sahr-oo-KOON-ee	At Angusaaruk's place
angusaaruungai	ah-ngoo-sahr-OON-gah-ee	Hi, Angusaaruk
aniapik	ahn-ee-ah-PEEK	my little brother
ataat	ah-TAHT	father (short form, similar to "dad")
ataata	ah-TAH-tah	father
ataatatsiak	ah-TAH-taht-see-ahk	grandfather (Inuttitut dialect spelling)
atii	ah-TEE	let's go
Atii qialirit	ah-TEE qee-ah-lee-reet	Go cry then.
Atiqaqquujingimmat	ah-TEE-kak-koo-yee-ngeem-mat	I don't think this place has a name.
atungatsaq	aht-oon-GAHT-sahk	thick skin of bearded seals used for the soles of sealskin boots
aujaq	AH-oo-yahk	summer
iglu	EEG-loo	snow house
ii	EE	yes
iilaak	EE-lahk	I know, or yes it is
iiqai	EE-kah-ee	I guess so, perhaps
ijirait	ee-YEE-rah-eet	shadow people (plural)
innirviit	EEN-neer-veet	wood frames for stretching sealskins
inukpasugjuit	EE-nook-pas-soog-joo-eet	mythological race of great giants, can be massive, nearly the size of moutains

Inummarialuulaurmat	EE-noom-mah-ree-ah-loo-lah-oor-maht	He was a real Inuk.
inummarik	EE-noom-mahr-eek	they lived like the old ways, like an Elder
Inuttitut	EE-noo-tee-toot	Inuktut language spoken in Nunavik and Labrador
inuujaq	EE-noo-yaq	traditional dolls made of driftwood (when said, "q" is silent)
iqaqti	EE-kahk-tee	black sealskin leather
ittuq	EE-took	Grandfather, or old man
Ivvilli?	EEV-vee-lee	What about you?
kajjait	kah-ee-JAH-EET	cursed wolves that travel in huge packs and have a hunger that cannot be sated
kamiik	kah-MEEK	two skin boots
kamiit	kah-MEET	many skin boots
Kaugjagjuk	kah-oog-JAHG-jook	A mistreated orphan from Inuit Mythology.
Kinakkunnik angijuqqaaqaravit?	kee-NAHK-oo-Neek ahn-gee-yooK-KAH-kah-rah-veet	Who are your parents?
Kinauvit?	kee-NAH-oo-veet	What is your name?
maktaaq	mahk-TAHK	Sliced narwhal or beluga skin, often with a bit of blubber attached
Mamianaugaluaq	mah-mee-AH-nah-oo-gah-LOO-AHK	I'm sorry, but . . .
Maniittuq	mah-NEET-ook	place name
Matukauqturuk	mah-too-KAH-OOK-too-rook	Hurry, close the door.

Miali Kalasimasi	mee-AH-lee kah-lah-see-MAH-see	Merry Christmas
naluaq	nah-loo-AHK	sealskin leather that was freeze-dried white in the winter
Nunamiinngaaqtuit	noo-naa-MEEN-NGAHK-too-EET	anything that comes from the land (plural)
Nunamiinngaaqtut	noo-nah-MEEN-NGAHK-toot	anything that comes from the land
panik	PAH-neek	daughter
paunnait	PAH-oon-nah-eet	drawf fireweed
piujuq	pee-OO-yook	it's beautiful
qallunaaq	kah-loo-NAHK	a white person
qallunaat	kah-loo-NAHT	white people
Qallunaatitut	kah-loo-NAH-ee-toot	the English langauge
qallupilluit	kah-loo-PEEL-loo-eet	myhological sea creatures that steal children through ice cracks
qamutiik	KAH-moo-teek	sled
qamutiit	KAH-moo-teet	sleds
qanuai	qah-NOO-ah-ee	it's like . . .
qanuinngittiaqtunga	kah-noo-EEN-NGEET-TII-AHK-toon-gah	I'm wonderful
qanukiaq	koo-noo-KEE-AHK	I'm not sure.
qarmait	KAHR-mah-eet	many sod houses (in dialogue, characters use "qarmaqs" to show how English plurals are at times used in speech by Inuktut speakers)
qavvik	KAHV-veek	wolverine

qijuktaaq	KEE-yook-tahk	Arctic heather
qujannamiik	koo-YAH-nah-meek	thank you
qulliq	KOO-leek	oil lamp
qunguliq	KOON-goo-leek	mountain sorrel
Quviasugit Quviasuvvingmit	KOOV-ee-ah-soo-geet KOOV-ee-ah-soo-veeng-meet	Merry Christmas (traditional Inuktitut phrasing)
Quviasuvviksiuriaqtunga	KOOV-see-ah-soo-VEEK-see-oo-ree-ah-toon-gah	I came here for Chirstmas.
Sanna	sah-NAH	Refers to a powerful mythological being, known as the mother of the sea mammals.
saattuujaaq	SAH-too-yaah	a stir-fry of carbou meat and onions (when said, "q" is silent)
Sauniapiingai	SAH-oon-ee-ah-peen-gah-ee	Hello, my namesake.
sauniq	SAH-oo-neek	a namesake
Sugami tamaaniikkit?	soong-mah-ee tah-MAH-NEEP-eet	What are you doing here?
Sugami tappaannialuk illuqaqpit?	soong-mah-ee tah-PAA-nee-AH-look ee-LOO-KAHK-peet	Why is your house way at the top of a cliff?
Suliviit?	soo-lee-VEET	Really?
suuqaima	SOO-kah-ee-MAH	Because
tah	TAH	exclamation
Taikunngaunngillutit	tah-ee-koo-NGAU-NGEEL-oo-LOO-teet	Don't go there.
taima	TAH-ee-mah	the end; enough

Takukannilaarivuguk.	TAHK-ook-ahn-nee-lah-ree-voo-goot	We will see each other again.
taannattauq	TAHN-aht-tah-ook	this one included
Tarnikuluk	TAHR-neek-oo-look	little soul
tarriaksuit	tah-REE-AHK-soo-EET	peaceful invisible race of beings (shadow people)
tavvauvutit	tah-VAH-OO-voo-teet	goodbye
tukiqanngi	took-ee-KAHN-NGEE	crazy, out of their mind
Tukisivinngaa?	took-see-vee-NGAH	Do you understand me?
Tuktumi takuvit tappaani?	took-too-MEE tah-koo-VEET tah-PAH-nee	Do you see a caribou up here?
Tusaaviit?	too-SAH-VEET	Are you listening?
Tusaaviuk?	too-SAH-vee-OOK	Do you hear it?
Tusaqsauvungaa?	too-SAHK-sah-oo-voo-NGAH	Can you hear me?
ukiaq	OO-kee-ahk	fall
ukiuq	OO-kee-ook	winter
uluit	OO-loo-eet	plural of "ulu," a crescent-shaped knife traditionally used by women
unaruluk	oo-nah-roo-LOOK	this senseless one
Upanngillugit	oo-pan-NGEEL-oo-geet	Don't approach them.
upirngaaq	oop-EER-NGAHK	spring
upirngassaaq	oo-PEER-NGah-SAHK	early spring
utirululaurit	oo-tee-roo-loo-LAH-OO-rEET	go back
Uvannulli tunnitit piujualuit.	oo-VAHN-oo-LEE toon-NEE-TEET pee-OO-yoo-AH-loo-EET	To me, your tattoos are beautiful.

Acknowledgments

Qujannamiik, thank you, for reading this collection of short stories. In my heart, I have three homes. Igloolik, where I grew up. Quaqtaq, my mom's hometown, where I'd go to visit my grandparents and where my ancestors are from. Lastly, Iqaluit, where I live now.

This collection, I think, is my ode to the loved ones I have lost over the last twenty-five years or so. In this way, I am able to tell them I love them one more time. My grandmothers, my late grandpa, my namesakes, aunts, uncles, cousins, my child-hood friends, the friends I've made along the way, and many more. I didn't expect to write so much about grief, but as an Inuk, we start grieving pretty early on in life. There are some people I have been mourning much longer than I knew them, and much longer than they were alive. I love them and I miss them. Ugh.

Some of these stories have already appeared in other publications:

"Maniittuq" was published in *Taaqtumi: An Anthology of Arctic Horror Stories, Vol. 2* in 2025.

"Tarnikuluk" won the 2014 Indigenous Arts and Stories award, as well as a Governor General's History Award, and is available to read on our-story.ca. However, in the time since I first wrote this story I have changed and grown, and don't necessarily agree with the first version I wrote, so I have edited it for this collection.

"Earring Repair Shop" appeared in issue 46.3 Ghosts of *Room* magazine. Thank you to Rachel Thompson for the invitation to contribute and for editing the initial version that appeared in the magazine.

I have so much gratitude and appreciation for Neil, Louise, and Danny, and everyone at Inhabit Media. A very heartfelt thank you to Kelly Ward-Wills, editor extraordinaire. Without Kelly's patience and gentle-handed approach, this collection might have collected dust for several more years.

I want to especially thank my family. My parents, Glen and Elisapee, who have been the most supportive and eager to read what comes next, and a little extra special thank you to my mum for going over the Inuttitut in "Mussels and Qunguliq" to make sure it was accurate in her dialect. Thank you to my siblings, Alannah and Anguti, my forever best friends since I was born. And of course, I have to thank Sunny, I just love him so much and he's the most polite dog anyone would ever come across.

Thank you to my friends Zorga, Robyn, Jackie, Marley, David, and Reena for all the ways you support me. As well, the friends I made during my time working at Ilitaqsiniq, especially to Jonah, Paj, Lily, Adriana, Kelly, Aliisa, and Panikuluk. I learned so much from you all and have grown so much in my journey to reclaim and revitalize my culture with your help.

Okay, for real, last and certainly not least, thank you to Stacey, Alethea, Moriah, and Garry. After years of taking time off from writing, working with you folks truly brought back my passion for storytelling and helped me to overcome whatever hurdles that were blocking my way before.

I have been so fortunate to have a community who supports me and pushes me to continue in my creative passion. It is hard to truly convey how much I appreciate you all. Qujannamiik.

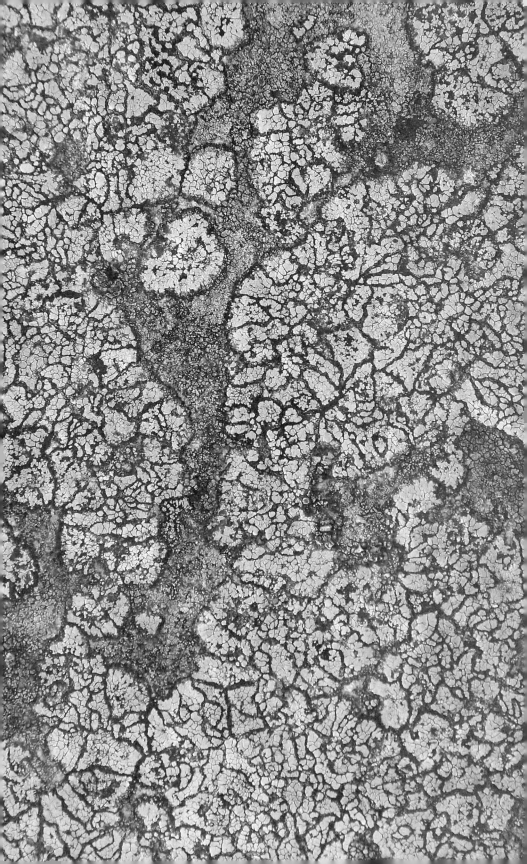

About the Author

Aviaq Johnston is an Inuk author who grew up in Igloolik, Nunavut. She has written the award-winning novel *Those Who Run in the Sky* (2017) and its sequel, *Those Who Dwell Below* (2019). Since winning the Indigenous Arts and Stories Award for her short story "Tarnikuluk" in 2014, Aviaq has explored many different styles of fiction writing, including children's picture books, young adult novels, short stories, and screenwriting for film and television. She lives in Iqaluit, Nunavut, with her dog, Sunny.

Iqaluit · Toronto